Wyld Wynd
The Unrest

Book Two of the Wyld Wynd Series

Peter Sandor

Wyld Wynd The Unrest, 3rd Edition.

05-10-25, REV 18

ISBN 978-0-9917954-6-8

Copyright 2019 by Peter Sandor

Read other books by Peter Sandor

<u>The Wyld Wynd Trilogy</u>

Book 1 – Wyld Wynd The Rising

Book2 – Wyld Wynd The Unrest

Book 3 – Wyld Wynd Unleashed

The Wall Plug Boys, a hilarious adult comedy

<u>The Talus 3 Series</u>

Book 1 – Arctic EMP

Book 2 – Galactic Illusions

Book 3 – Forsaken Drifter

Book 4 – Time Undone

Paperbacks, hardcovers and ebooks are available from Amazon.

Contents

Chapter 1   1

Chapter 2   15

Chapter 3   28

Chapter 4   35

Chapter 5   47

Chapter 6   55

Chapter 7   60

Chapter 8   73

Chapter 9   80

Chapter 10   84

Chapter 11   100

Chapter 12   106

Chapter 13   116

Chapter 14   125

Chapter 15   134

Chapter 1

Nolan slept for over eight hours until his eyes finally opened to the drab, gray ceiling of the room he occupied. Instantly, his recollection went to the panic of the freefall. His mind vividly remembered the image of his flailing body careening over the cliff. With some surprise, the only pain he felt was in his head, as he turned his face toward the light beaming through the plate-glass window to his left. He propped himself up on his elbows expecting now, as he moved his hands, to surely feel pain. Then, as he turned his head to the right in a wide, stretching arc, he moved each of his legs, wincing at the expected pain that again didn't come. His recollection of the cliff was sharp, but from the time he felt Daniel's hand on his shoulder, the memory blurred until it went altogether blank. He realized he must have escaped the rocks. He had made his first planer hop, and he was alive.

It was through the narrowed eye slits of the less than becoming wince that his gaze fell on Germaine, sitting in a liberally-cushioned chair to his right.

"I feel like I've been hit by a bus," Nolan said with a raspy voice. He surveyed his surroundings from the thin bed he lay on. The room was small with only one large window and a door on the wall to his right. The four walls were painted a bright-yellow, and there was one picture hanging on the wall opposite to him. It, along with the window and door, were the only breaks in the sea of yellow.

Germaine sat forward, a smug grin on his face. "Well, honestly, with that look on your face, you look like you have been hit by a bus."

Nolan's lips turned into a frown. Clearing his throat, he responded. "Perhaps you haven't looked in a mirror." The warrior's face was still swollen and had a small bandage on the cut over his left eye. Before Germaine could respond, Nolan asked, "Where's Daniel?" His voice was suddenly anxious with concern.

"Fear not. Daniel is fine. He'll be away for a few days visiting a friend, and he has left you in my charge: welcoming wagon, tour guide and bodyguard, all in one."

Nolan straightened his arms, lifting himself further off the bed, then he slung his legs off the side. His hand came up to his head, rubbing his temple. "My head is pounding."

At the same moment, the door to the room was pushed open. A young woman, clad in a cream-colored dress, strode in. She looked at Germaine briefly before smiling at Nolan. She noticed Nolan's fingers at his head and moved over to the small table beside the bed. Picking up the two pills from the light-green colored tabletop with one hand and the glass of water with the other, she turned to Nolan. "Take these. They'll make you feel much better."

Glancing at Germaine over the woman's shoulder, Nolan saw his curt nod. He popped both pills, then lifted the glass, letting the water chase them to his stomach. He noticed the woman's subtle accent, finding it similar to Daniel's. Other than that, she seemed the same as a typical woman of Earth, except she was wearing very little make-up, and her jet-black hair was cut quite short.

The woman, who Nolan now realized was a nurse, moved to a stand-up cupboard situated against the far wall. He was surprised to feel the pain in his head was clearing up almost immediately. As it did so, he became more aware of his surroundings and noticed he was not dressed in his clothes. A thin, white, cotton shirt covered his upper body, while a like-colored pair of loose shorts was all he wore below his waist. He looked at Germaine, asking, "Where are my clothes?"

The woman came back into Nolan's line of sight, carrying a brown parchment parcel. "These are your clothes," she said, barely above a whisper. "All new immigrants are processed here at this center. They are inspected for any sign of disease and cleaned." Her face blushed to a glowing pink.

Nolan saw Germaine's smug grin was still on his chiseled face. Then, he turned his eyes back to the woman as awkward seconds of silence seemed like minutes. His subconscious told him to cross his legs, so he did.

The uncomfortable quiet was broken by the woman. "The last thing we need to do is a blood test." Her voice trailed off as she moved toward a medical cabinet across the room.

Germaine pulled himself to his feet. "That won't be necessary. We did an off-world test. Here are the results." Reaching into his coat pocket, he pulled out a folded paper and held it out to the nurse.

As she walked over, the woman frowned, taking the paper and unfolding it under her olive-colored eyes. She shook her head, mumbling to herself, the side-to-side movements became more insistent. "No, this won't do. We have our rules. All immigrants must be processed, and that includes a blood test here." She folded up the paper and matter-of-factly pushed it back toward Germaine.

Germaine reached into the same pocket for a second time, pulling out a small laminated card. He held it out in front of the woman for her to easily see. "My authorization supersedes your protocol." With a smile, he pressed the paper, still in the woman's hand, back toward her with the tip of his index finger.

As she saw the card, her thin eyebrows rose in surprise. Leaning forward, she inspected it a second time, then did a double-take at Germaine. Composing herself, she pulled in the paper and put it in the side pocket of her dress. "Yes, Sir. He's released then. You'll need to sign for him on the way out through the security checkpoint." With that, she curtly turned and strode out of the room.

Nolan's fingers moved to open the parcel, but he was curious in that there was a flicker of relief in Germaine's eyes.

"No, Nolan." Germaine walked over to the same upright cupboard the woman retrieved the parcel from and pulled out an assortment of clothing. "You might want to wear these. Remember, you're on the world of Crann Bith now, and you need to dress the part." He draped the clothes on the bed before turning toward the door. "I'll wait for you outside."

Nolan heard the gentle tap of the door against the frame, leaving him alone with his thoughts. He pushed the fingers from both hands back through his hair. His head was now devoid of pain, replaced by a sense of anxiety hidden from Germaine while he was in the room. What was he doing? he thought. He left Earth with death in his wake at every step. Now, he was on another world he knew nothing about, and he didn't even know why he was here. Daniel had given him an abundance of information about the war and the pureblood castes of men who fought in it. The thought of adventure intrigued him, and he thought that was enough to overcome any semblance of fear. However, now that he was here and alone for the first time in several days, he felt the fear course through his veins, causing his brow to break out in a sweat. He closed his eyes and took the deep breaths he'd learned would relax him. He hoped now, since he was headlong into the adventure of life, he could, at a minimum, keep his cool. But he knew there was more than just that to his presence here. He felt it in his gut. There was an unknown part he had yet to play. Daniel brought him here, but he sensed Daniel was also just a player in a bigger game. Although he felt the confusion and the apprehension of being in a new world, he had an ironic feeling. It was an even stronger sense this was where he belonged. He didn't know the specifics, but in time he would. He just hoped he could live up to the expectation of Daniel and the others around him, but even more so, he needed to live up to his own expectations.

Needing a distraction, Nolan inspected the clothes. He pulled the jacket off the hanger, holding it up in front of himself. It was made of pitch-black, very thin leather and had no buttons. Rather, it had a like-colored belt slung through three loops at the waist of the thigh-length coat. Placing the coat down, he dressed quickly after finding boxer style underpants and thin socks. Next, he pulled on the slacks. They were also black, thin and loose-fitting. The material was unusual to him. It felt like cotton, but had a shine to it almost as if silken threads were woven in with the cotton. Next was the shirt. He smiled, as it reminded him of the swashbucklers of old Earth. It was white with a loose, wide collar and baggy sleeves. Sewn in dark-green along a narrow band down the front center of the shirt, was an intricate pattern of tight swirls and intertwined lines resembling the branches of a rose bush. The same pattern was sewn around the cuffs, and there was one small, green leaf embroidered into each front corner of the flowing collar.

Nolan pulled the shirt on and did up the buttons as he walked over to the mirror mounted on the far wall. He turned his head slightly to the side as he looked at his reflection. Definitely different from Earth, he thought, but he could get used to it. His tall frame looked good in the stylish clothes.

Bending to the side, he looked in the clothes cupboard, spotting the black leather boots. Moving back to the bed, he sat and pulled each short boot on, smiling as he felt the comfortable fit. On each boot he closed the strap, held tight by the miracle of velcro that had apparently been discovered on this world also. He chuckled as he thought, some things just don't change, notwithstanding the distance between worlds or planes.

As he walked back to the mirror, he pulled on the jacket. It fit loosely, and the front was held closed by the belt bundled in a tight knot. He bent his knees as he went up and down, to and from a crouched position. The clothes gave a wide range of motion and a high degree of comfort. Now prepared for the day ahead, he walked to the door, opened it and approached Germaine who he saw just outside in the bright hallway, leaning against the wall.

As soon as Germaine saw him, his fingers moved to Nolan's shirt collar, straightening it. "The clothes fit well. The cute nurse took your measurements accurately," Germaine commented with a sly grin.

As Nolan opened his mouth to retort, Germaine said, "Watch."

Nolan lowered his gaze, watching Germaine undo the belt he just knotted and re-tie it in a different style. It wasn't complicated—just different, with the two short remaining ends of the belt left flat and down across his groin.

Germaine's eyes came up to Nolan's. "I'm not originally from this world, but they have their own unique customs here, so, for some reason, the knot has significance. The type of knot and the expertise in tying it clearly seems to mean something to these people. Remember what I just showed you, and you'll get by."

Nolan nodded his head, but Germaine had already turned and was striding down the hallway. His voice carried back to Nolan. "You must be hungry. Come along."

Nolan quickly followed, putting his observation skills into use. He noticed Germaine's clothes were similar to his, except his jacket was worn and the color faded at the elbows. Except for the color being a dark green, the style and fit of his pants were the same as what he wore. In fact, as they walked through the corridor, he noticed all the men were dressed in the same manner except for the varying color combinations. All in all, the men dressed smartly with a casual look. Only a few of them had a more official appearance marked by colored buttons along the front of the collar of their coats.

The women had a different aura about them. Most wore dresses while only a few wore slacks. For the most part, their clothing was tight fitting, accentuating their figures. It didn't take Nolan long to notice there was no one carrying a disproportioned body weight. Their walk was taking some time, and they passed at least 50 people, but he hadn't yet seen one overweight or overly thin person. He thought it curious, but put it to the back of his mind as he caught up to Germaine.

Realizing his breaths were unusually heavy, Nolan turned to the warrior. "The air is thinner on this world."

"Actually, it's not," Germaine replied without breaking his stride. "The gravity and air are similar here to your Earth, but we're at a high elevation. Shortly, you will see we are 8,000 feet above sea level. Similar to Earth, it will not take your body long to adjust to the modified conditions."

Nolan felt as if his lungs would burst. He wasn't used to this. Thankfully, their brisk walk was halted when they arrived at a gate protected by two security guards. Again, they were dressed in similar clothing, right down to the thin, loose-fitting, leather jackets. However, from head to toe their clothing was gray except for the two red buttons attached to the collar of the coat, and he assumed this signified a rank.

Nolan stayed in the background as Germaine showed them his credentials. From his position, he heard Germaine mention his name. As one of the security guards moved to a computer terminal, Germaine motioned Nolan forward with a wave of his hand.

The other guard looked at Nolan. "Stand on the white circle on the floor, and look at the camera."

It took only a few minutes for Nolan to be processed. He was given a security card with his picture on it. In addition, he signed a document agreeing to abide by the rules of the city of Bailemor. He noticed Daniel had previously signed the form, identifying himself as Nolan's sponsor. Germaine signed under Daniel's signature, as it was a prerequisite for his release from the complex.

The two guards said nothing more, watching Nolan warily as he and Germaine left the checkpoint through the two large, glass double-doors and into the courtyard flooded with the late morning sunlight.

"Welcome to Bailemor, capital and one of only two cities on Crann Bith," Germaine said, barely above his breath.

Nolan took small turning steps as he looked around his position. The large building behind him was eight stories high. It's what he now knew was an immigration and receiving complex. It was made of what appeared to be concrete but colored to a pinkish hue with a line of gray at the separation of each floor, giving the facade an aesthetically pleasing look. Turning further, another building, the same height as the first, bound the diamond-shaped courtyard along its opposite corner. It had the same construction and colors, but the front had two sides, angled at 90 degrees to match the courtyard's shape. Each long front wall, dotted with windows, took up the length of the courtyard in each direction.

The courtyard itself was marked by a series of crisscrossed walking pathways dotted with intermittent wooden benches, some complimented by colorful, adjoined tables. The red, crushed-gravel pathways further complimented the trees that boasted green and dark-purple leaves. What was interesting was the two colors of leaves adorned the same tree, yet they were different. The purple leaf was thin and spiny, while the green leaves were large, wide and flat.

Nolan realized he would have so many questions. Already, so many amassed in his mind, and he was only moments out the door. *At least the grass was a familiar green, although the blades were fat,* he thought as he bent down, touching the soft carpet of growth.

His mouth opened in amazement. He hadn't seen it until now, but as he looked over top of the blanket of green and purple leaves in the courtyard, through the opening between the buildings, there was a mountain. Even though it was quite a distance away, he could see it was covered in tri-colors of green, and the very top was tipped in white snow. Along the near edge, a great horizontal platform jutted out from the inclined mountainside. It was difficult to judge, partly because of the distance, but also from what he suspected was its less than believable enormity. From this position, the platform looked ten miles away, spanning a depth of another two miles to where it joined the mountainside. The man-made platform spread across the entire visible horizon within the view between the buildings. Underneath it, where there should have been shadows, there was light. *There must be an ingenious system of refracting devices,* he concluded as he looked in awe at the monumental stilts supporting the lower structure of the platform.

Nolan turned to Germaine. "That's freaking amazing."

"Yes, that would be the Upper City, but in your amazement, I hope you can still feel hunger. I certainly do, so let's go eat." Germaine turned, walking along one of the pathways through the courtyard toward the two-sided building.

Nolan followed in between the colorful trees and now saw the multitude of colorful flowers dotting the ground amongst the small, beautifully designed rock gardens. They entered the building, making their way to the sixth floor then out onto a patio on the far side of the building. This terrace, which had not been visible from Nolan's vantage point in the courtyard, was in the shape of a large semi-circle. It cantilevered from the side of the building with an extension curling around the back wall. Numerous tables and chairs dotted the decorative brick surface, and between them were small ornamental trees in large, wooden pots. All this provided Nolan with a very favorable first impression of his first off-world restaurant.

A young man met them as they arrived on the terrace and showed them to a table near the thick, sculptured, concrete railing. Germaine ordered two drinks, telling the waiter the food would be ordered shortly. As the waiter walked briskly back toward the building, Germaine pointed across the table over the railing and said, "There is a better view of the city from here."

Nolan shifted his chair and leaned over the railing. From this vantage point, six floors up, he had an even better view of the platform Germaine called the Upper City. But from this edge of the building, he could also see the city spread out in both directions, as far as the eye could see. What he saw was modern with taller buildings on his right, smaller buildings on his left. As his gaze scanned further to his left, he saw a greater abundance of green intermingled with the buildings and was relieved to see this world was more than just concrete and steel.

"The heart of the city is to your right. There's more agricultural land to your left," Germaine said, predicting Nolan's question.

Tilting his chin up at the platform in the distance, Nolan questioned, "Why do they call that the Upper Platform?"

"Because this is the Lower Platform," Germaine responded.

Nolan had a confused look on his face. "What do you mean? I only see one platform." He looked out again at the Upper Platform's enormity, seeing from this height the huge supporting stilts anchored into the sloped mountainside.

"Correct. That is the Upper Platform, or as we sometimes call it, the Upper City. The level we are on—the level this entire city is on, is actually the Lower City. We are on a platform supported 8,000 feet above sea level."

"That's impossible!" Nolan blurted out.

"Come with me for a moment while they get our drinks." Germaine rose, leading Nolan, who had a look of disbelief on his face, around the edge of the semi-circle until they were on the small portion of the veranda at the back of the building.

Germaine didn't have to say anything. Looking over the railing, there was a depth that Nolan had difficulty comprehending. Both hands firmly grasped the railing as the Earthman looked over the edge. Below them was a roadway at the base of the building, then 50 yards of what appeared to be shops on the other side. Beyond that was a tall block wall running in a curved line off into the distance in each direction until it faded into the haze of the horizon.

The wall was the edge of the Lower Platform Germaine had described. On the other side, was a drop of some one thousand feet to the ground below. Nolan realized, looking first behind him and then down once again, the declining rugged mountainside continued under the Lower City. Even though he could not see them, he surmised, under them, there must be thousands of the same massive, circular pylons he saw supporting the Upper

City.

Nolan saw the mountainside below their position was well forested, the trees finding every well-soiled nook between the numerous boulders and rocks speckling the terrain. In a few areas there were massive jutting cliffs with one having a long thin waterfall cascading over the edge. The water crashed into a small pool at the bottom that was difficult to see through the spray being thrust upward in curved, billowing currents of water vapor.

Across the spray, a colorful rainbow made nature's painting complete. One end of the rainbow was lost over the horizon while the other end curved downward in a great sweep, obscuring into the red fog below. Nolan frowned as his trance was broken by the less-than-artistic ending of red fog. He pointed his finger downward. "What's that?"

Germaine stood closer to Nolan. "That, unfortunately, is the red haze covering the surface of this planet. Some eight hundred years ago, there was a planet-wide war that almost destroyed every form of life. The red haze is what is left when people try to kill each other just for the sake of the killing itself." Germaine's voice became cold. "Hundreds of bombs were dropped. Some were meant to destroy people while others were made to seep into the soil and destroy the plant life. There were also sonic bombs, instantaneously flattening an 80-mile diameter from its epicenter. When the people were dead and the plant life faded to nothing, all that was left was the red, poisonous haze slowly swirling over the surface of this world. It's a combination of the chemicals from the bombs mixed with the dust created when soil is devoid of plant life."

Nolan looked out over the red haze that was such a contrast to this city and the mountain supporting it. In the distance the fog was thick, but he still saw some green intermingled in one zone. "What's over there?" he asked, his finger pointing toward what seemed an anomaly.

"You have good eyes," the warrior said through a chuckle. His cold demeanor faded with Nolan's continued curiosity. "The plant life is resilient. Little by little, the planet comes back to life. After the holocaust, the trees tried to grow, yet they died, but the seed lived on and each time adapted—each time becoming hardier, and each time they grew a little higher toward the sky before dying. The patch of trees you see is a group of some 200 trees, and each is over 300 feet high. They have—and I'm not sure if this is the right word for it—*mutated* to what they are today. Their trunks are easily sixty yards across at the base as they shoot skywards over the red haze, throwing out a thick carpet of green foliage above the harmful gases. As such, they survive. There are more than a few such isolated forests on the surface of this planet.

"The haze at the foot of the mountain is thinner than that further out. Why?"

"I stand corrected," Germaine responded. "At the foot of the mountain is a great wide plateau. The haze dissipates with elevation. That's why we are clear of its evils here. The plateau has an elevation of 800 feet. As such, it's not altogether free of the poisonous gases, but it is somewhat bearable."

"How can any type of poison gas be bearable in any way?"

Germaine took a deep breath before answering. "Centuries ago, when the first remaining purebloods came out of their underground lairs, they knew they could only survive in the clean air of the higher altitudes. After this extended amount of time, as the planet is slowly cleansing itself, the red haze is not readily lethal. For example, an average pureblood of Bailemor, if not killed in the war, might well live to his 80's. If he lived down on the surface at sea level, assuming he found safe food and water, he might live to 30. On the plateau, the same man might live to be 50. So, the red haze will not kill you right away, but the slow chemical affects, over time, will decrease your life expectancy."

The waiter came over to their position. "Your drinks have been at the table for some time," he said with a nervous smile.

Both men took a deep breath of air in unison, perhaps spurred on by their conversation playing on their subconscious. Nolan took a step toward the waiter, but stopped in his tracks. In his intoxication with the beautiful mountainside that slid into the red haze, he didn't notice, directly across from them, a second mountain with a second city. He spun around quickly, doing a 360-degree rotation. To his far right was a third mountain city in the distance.

Germaine's voice cleared up Nolan's confusion. "Bailemor is, in fact, a city covering this mountain, and the mountain has three peaks."

Nolan continued his steps toward their table. "I think I need that drink, and I hope it's alcoholic," he muttered.

An older woman came over to their table, wearing tight pants and a close-fitting top, making it difficult not to notice her full breasts. Germaine ordered the meal, saving Nolan the folly of even more questions. For a time, there were no words between them. Nolan needed the time to absorb what he learned while he gazed out over the railing into the city, watching the people who walked the streets below them.

The waitress was back quickly with the food, placing a colorful, light-blue plate in front of each of them. Nolan enjoyed the flavor, surprisingly good for a simple looking meal. There was a small piece of meat, a salad and a piece of toasted bread on the plate. The bread was particularly tasty, having a spicy cheese spread on it.

Between bites, Nolan asked, "I couldn't help but notice the men and women on this world do not dress the same."

Leaning over the plate, Germaine's eyes looked up. "That should not be that unusual. Men and women are different."

"Of course, men and women are different, but every man I've seen has loose fitting clothes, while all the women—every one has tight fitting clothes." Nolan pushed his point.

Finished eating, Germaine leaned back and pulled the napkin from his lap, tossing it casually on his plate. "I've been to many planes and many worlds. Although there are a few, and I mean a very few exceptions, there's one thing consistent to each—that being the male in the species is dominant." He waved his hand to and fro. "I know—I know. On many worlds my words would be considered chauvinistic, but look at nature. In almost every case, the male is dominant. Then consider women, and I do understand that not all women are the same, but most appear to enjoy wearing clothing which highlights their figure."

Nolan chuckled. "You chauvinist."

"All I tell you is what nature puts in front of your eyes, but you do not see. I assume the women on your planet wear high heels. I say that only because on all the worlds I've been to, there have not been many where I haven't seen high heels. Is that because they're more comfortable?" He laughed. "No, that is not true, otherwise I believe you and I would be wearing them. Women wear high heels because it accentuates the look of their legs and, in particular, the calf muscles. They know men enjoy that."

Nolan just shook his head in disbelief.

"The same can be said for low cut tops, or shirts showing a woman's midriff, or hip-hugging pants. Are these worn for comfort? What about make-up? Trust me, my young friend, women don't wear it for protection from the sun." Germaine leaned forward. "Women do all these things because men enjoy it. The interplay between men and women is written into their genes and is a natural part of being human. It has been so from the dawn of time."

Nolan looked at Germaine for a few seconds, a wry smile on his face. He didn't respond. He didn't dare tell Germaine his initial question was not a complaint—just an observation.

Having finished lunch, the two men left the restaurant. Germaine gave the waiter his security card on the way out, whereby Nolan learned the card also doubled as a credit card.

As they made their way back down to the courtyard, Germaine said, "It's only a 15-minute walk from here to Daniel's accommodations. For now, that's where you and I will be staying."

Nolan nodded, following the warrior as they traversed down the few steps from the courtyard, before making a left turn onto a smoothly-bricked sidewalk. From this level, the city was even more appealing. One could see there was great care taken in the tasks performed by the inhabitants, but even more so by the workers of Bailemor. The streets were clean, and wherever Nolan looked, at the colorful buildings or the street-side benches and lampposts, there was a quaint feeling to this part of the city. The numerous flower arrangements hanging from rails overtop of the street and in pots alongside the sidewalk, gave proof to the obvious consideration for detail.

As fascinated as Nolan was by the cityscape supported by the platform of concrete and steel, it was the people who captivated his interest. He looked into their faces, seeing most carrying wide smiles. The war had been a steady item for all their lives, and they lived through it while accepting it as a necessity. Nonetheless, most appeared as though they were happy in spite of it.

The pair made a turn onto another wide side-street. Almost immediately Nolan heard a reverberation coming from further along the roadway. It became louder as it came closer to their position. He shifted his gaze toward the source of the noise to see five lines of men come from around a corner ahead of them. There was a loud order barked from one of the men marching at the side of the troupe, and instantly, they were at a trot coming down the roadway toward their position.

Nolan stopped, tugging on Germaine's jacket. "I want to watch this."

Germaine obliged, stopping beside Nolan. "They're a *Sword Squad*—a division of our military. You see the blue tassel hanging from the back of their helmets?"

Nolan nodded.

"They are the Akkadian Blue Swords," Germaine clarified.

Half of the troupe was already past their position. Nolan saw they wore the same loose pants, shirts and leather jackets. All were a midnight-blue— in fact, almost black in color. There were belts slung around their waists, and attached to each was another belt angling across their chests. It wrapped over their shoulders, angling down their backs to rejoin the belt at their waists. Hanging from the waist belts was a holster supporting a pistol. Hanging from the belts at their back were sheaths, and in each was a short, curved sword, easily accessible by a hand pushed back over the shoulder. Some of the men had short hair, some longer, under midnight-blue, metal helmets. Each curved down to cover the cheekbones with the rest of the face being left exposed. From there the helmets, buffed to a perfect sheen, curved down to cover the ear and the side of the neck before squaring off at collar length. There was a small metal button on the crown of the helmets, at the rear. From these hung the foot-long, blue tassels, reminding Nolan of a show horse's tail. The warriors looked ominous in their completely dark attire with the only color being in the tassels and the hilt of their swords. These were a bright sea-blue. They looked sharp.

The sound of their stomping feet dissipated in the distance as the troupe made quick double-time.

"An interesting combination of weapons," Nolan offered. "Pistols and swords."

"When you are involved in a war played out over numerous worlds, having an even wider variety of laws and customs, you best be familiar with all forms of warfare," Germaine replied.

"It seems this world is well prepared for war. In our short walk, I noticed two batteries of anti-aircraft guns. They were well disguised, but they were there. Also, in the distance between two buildings, I saw what I first thought was a barricaded construction site, but by the look of the buildings surrounding it and the shape of the pit, it appeared to me to be a bomb crater. I hope your warriors fight as good as they look."

"You are very observant, Nolan. You see much another would not notice." Germaine looked directly into Nolan's eyes. "I wonder if that is a curse or a blessing?"

Nolan looked away as he continued striding alongside the bigger man. He thought it was a good question. There were times he didn't wish he was so perceptive. Even now, he couldn't get the troupe of warriors out of his mind. They had looked noble in their sharp dress, but that wasn't what he would remember of the first military group he viewed on Bailemor. Rather, etched in his memory would be the fear he saw living in their young eyes.

Chapter 2

It was mid-morning. Germaine and Nolan, having just left Daniel's house, were walking along the street toward a set of stairs visible just ahead through the light, falling rain. They angled down from the sidewalk to an underground level. Nolan, well refreshed from a trouble-free night of sleep, took light steps down the stairs as he followed Germaine.

The previous night, Germaine showed Nolan some of the more menial aspects of Bailemor life. This included an explanation of the fridge, the food cupboard and the contents described with an overabundance of detail. Some of the items were comparable to earth foods while, for a few others, Nolan put a mental image of a big, red X over them.

Germaine also showed Nolan the video receiver where he could watch different types of programs. Nolan paid close attention. As much as he appreciated Germaine's explanations, if the video receiver was even somewhat similar to the television systems on Earth, he was confident he would spend quite a bit of time in front of it, both for the purposes of entertainment and education. The last item Nolan put to memory was the computer situated in a small room converted to an office. Germaine gave him a brief lesson on its use. With it, Nolan could increase his knowledge, not only of Crann Bith, but the history of the great pureblood races. He chuckled. If only Microsoft knew of the market share they were missing.

Nolan was given his own room in Daniel's house. It was spacious and stylishly appointed with warm colors. The closet along the side of the room had several hanging jackets and slacks while shirts filled the confines of a wooden chest situated at the foot of the bed. The clothes were all similar to those he'd been given the previous day. However, the similarity ended in the general design, as the varied colors and materials made each a unique arrangement.

Daniel's house was a surprise to Nolan. First, it wasn't actually a house, but a large apartment on the second floor of a building encompassing many such living accommodations. He had always considered Daniel to be rustic and weathered. As such, he expected the older man's taste to be old fashioned, yet his accommodations were quite the opposite with fashionable colors and a touch of upper-crust detail in every room. There were more than a few art pieces—from modern freeform clay carvings, to oil paintings, to several pieces of furniture that were wonderfully restored antiques. In Nolan's opinion there was a touch of class and style to the dwelling not fitting the character of the older man he'd come to know.

Nolan stopped daydreaming in time to readjust his feet coming off the bottom step of the stairs. They made a turn at the bottom, coming to face a plate-glass door where Nolan momentarily evaluated his reflection. He was clad in the same clothing as the day before except for the white shirt which was replaced with one of bright yellow, tastefully embroidered with black vertical threads at the cuffs and collar.

Germaine swiped his security card through the reader, and the thick door swung inward with a rattle. His demeanor so far this morning was quiet. For a man of few words, he'd spoken many the day before. Today, he would let Nolan's eyes and ears be the primary mode for his learning exercises.

Nolan thought the hallway on the other side of the door was no different from the underground areas under any apartment complex of Earth, looking like it needed a fresh coat of paint. He followed Germaine along the well-lit hallway to a series of elevators where Germaine pushed the button on the front of the first elevator. The door slid open with the prompt, and they stepped in. Tapping his knuckles on the wall, Nolan realized the two walls, floor and the ceiling were a thin layer of plexiglass. However, this plexiglass was only an inner skin, fitting inside a similar sized steel enclosure. The compartment was not that large, and at the end opposite to their entry was another closed sliding door. This was also made of the same clear plexiglass.

The numeric keypad on the side wall was within Germaine's reach. He keyed in the sequence 32F6, and when his finger hit the *end* sequence key, the entire inner plexiglass housing shifted forward, out of the steel enclosure, settling onto two iron forks Nolan hadn't previously noticed.

Now able to see out in all directions from the plexiglass housing, Nolan saw they were in an underground garage. In front of them was a bank of storage compartments, three-high and twenty-wide, divided by a grid-work of black, steel beams with a yellow light marking each intersection where the steel was joined with giant bolts.

Germaine finally spoke as the plexiglass container, supported by the forks, traveled toward stall 32F6. "Bullet cars are what we use for transportation under the city." He angled his eyes upward. "Most of the stalls have a bullet parked in them." He pointed his finger toward the grid-work. "They're electric and travel on a system of monorails, guided by the city's traffic computers."

The plexiglass housing came to a stop in front of a stall on the third level. This time the inner, glass door swung open, allowing them to step onto a grated, metal catwalk. The vehicle within the stall was cylindrical with an aerodynamic, bullet-shaped nose at each end. The top half of the bullet was made of curved plexiglass with molded reinforcing bars surrounding the cylindrical shape, while the bottom was molded of a hard polymer compound. As Nolan was beginning to realize, the people of Bailemor liked bright colors. This bullet was metallic-silver with two thin, red stripes along the entire length of the vehicle. There was a small, round, bright-blue circle painted on this side of the car near the back and just above the double stripe.

Nolan was still admiring the bullet when Germaine pushed the button on a remote-control he'd pulled from his coat pocket. A sharp, audible beep was emitted, and simultaneously, a red light began to strobe across a bar on the side of the car. A crack appeared as a door pushed open and slid aft, providing access to the passenger compartment.

"After you," Germaine said.

There were six seats, and each was on a central support anchored to the carpeted floor. They were covered in a durable fabric with the red color matching the stripes on the outside of the vehicle. Nolan gingerly stepped into the vehicle which gave it a gentle rock, as it hung from the central support attaching it to the overhead monorail. Feeling the motion and unsure of himself, he quickly pressed his frame into the far central chair.

Germaine followed Nolan into the bullet, lowering himself into a seat at the front of the car with a casualness indicating his experience with the vehicle. He patted the seat beside him. "Come. Sit beside me, so you can see what I'm doing." Germaine's fingers slid over a computer console set on an angle at the front of the compartment. His hand grazed a yellow button on the left side of a wide keypad. Once again, the red light pulsed across the bar at the top of the door as it slid forward and sealed tight.

Nolan pressed his frame into the chair beside his temporary tutor. He saw Germaine pull a harness-style seat belt across his chest, and he followed suit after finding a similar device attached to his chair. Germaine was already in his teaching mode, and Nolan was becoming used to it as he now began his second full day with the warrior. Germaine was more to the point than Daniel, but his monotone voice required Nolan to increase his concentration, so he would not lose focus.

Hitting several keys with agile fingers, Germaine began the lesson for the day. "Each of the bullet cars in the city is connected to the city's computers via the electrical connection through the monorail." He nonchalantly pointed a finger upward for a moment. "The computer then does most of the work, tracking each vehicle and ensuring each gets to its destination in the most efficient and safe manner." Light clicks were audible as he pressed in a sequence of key strokes. "I'm typing in our present location, our destination and the recommended path. As an alternative, if I wasn't sure of the best path, I could ask for one from the computer's memory." With that, eight lines of text appeared on the video display terminal. A message came across the bottom of the screen – *approved*, and they jerked forward, as the bullet was pulled from the stall via a three-axis crane. On the video display the top line of their route remained solid while the other seven lines were flashing. In the top right corner of the screen a number *5* also flashed.

Pointing to the *5*, Nolan asked, "What's that?"

"That's our position in the cue to the chute," Germaine replied. "There are four other bullets ahead of us, ready to leave this station." He flicked a toggle switch on the console, and a round radar screen crackled to life. On it appeared a colorful plan view of the station with their car at the center of the display. Nolan could see the other four bullets as flashing blue dots on different areas of the screen. Three were in line to a common point while the fourth, similar to their own progress, was in transit.

The crane finished its horizontal movement, stopping with a jolt before lowering three levels to the chute entry. Once there, Nolan saw only one black bullet in front of them, and the number in the top righthand corner of the video screen had changed to a *2*. Angling his face upward, he could see the thick monorail above them providing support, energy and communication. The monorail was actually incorrectly named. Looking closely, he could see a double rail with a primary and, above it, a second redundant rail. The grapple attached to the top of the bullet rode on the first rail. Just above it was a second grapple with clearance to the second rail. He could see that, in the event of a failure of the primary rail or grapple, the bullet would drop an inch until it caught the second rail, and he assumed an emergency brake would be applied. *Ingenious*, he thought as he heard a whirling sound begin to build up. It peaked as the brake on the car in front of them was released, shooting the car forward along the rail.

Nolan grinned. "This is going to be fun." He rubbed his hands together in anticipation.

Their silver bullet inched forward, then came to a stop. Almost immediately, a light on the console began to flash red numerals, counting down from 5. When the countdown came to zero their silver bullet shot forward, causing their speed to build as the acceleration rate grew. The white lights illuminating the underground area appeared as flashes to the two passengers as the bullet screamed along the rail.

Looking ahead, Nolan could see the rail and lights curl to the right and down. A brighter light could be seen on the other side of a concrete wall blocking their view of the rail from that point onward. Almost before the thought was completed, his head was pushed to the left with the G-force of the turn, notwithstanding the bullet's 45-degree pitch forced by their momentum. Before the turn was finished, the rail angled downward. Both passengers were pressed up against the straps holding them in place as the bullet continued to speed down the rail. The Earthman's knuckles were white, as his hands clutched the arms of the chair.

Nolan managed to lift one hand to shield his eyes from the bright light bathing the bullet as soon as they began the turn. Suddenly, they burst through the opening in the bottom of the platform and into bright daylight. His stomach lurched into his throat as his body stressed against the straps. At the same time, he blinked several times as his pupils dilated to the new light level. Once adjusted, his eyes opened wide as soon as he discovered he was traveling one thousand feet above the rugged mountainside below. Eventually, he looked at the console, relieving his momentary feeling of vertigo as their speed settled at 110 miles an hour. His mind reacted quickly, comprehending how the rail had swept down to the underside of the lower platform. Their bullet began a wide-arced sweep until their direction was almost due west as indicated by the compass in the car's front console.

"Freaking hell—that was a rush!" Nolan looked down through the curved window. Behind them he saw the massive pylon they just left. His eyes scanned under the expanse of the platform, seeing many other pylons with a typical spacing of some five hundred yards. Germaine flicked another toggle switch, and the radar's resolution changed, backing out to a wider view. Their bullet stayed at the center of the display, and Nolan could see other blue, flashing dots, representing other bullets all around them on various rails.

Germaine turned his eyes to look at Nolan, seeing his excitement. He grinned as he noticed the blood hadn't altogether returned to the Earthman's face. "You'll get used to the bullet cars. They're actually quite safe, and there are very few accidents," Germaine said in the most comforting voice he could muster through the smug grin.

"Where are we going?" Nolan asked after a few minutes.

"The Military Sector is on the west side of the city, and within it is the Skills Academy where they shall determine when they can fit you in. Most of your time for the next few months will be spent there, where you will be taught academics, self-defense and the use of your psychic powers." Germaine hit a switch on the side of his seat, unlocking it. His feet pushed on the blue carpet under him, and the chair rotated to face Nolan.

Nolan was a quick study. He did the same, rotating his own seat and gently rocked himself in an arc back and forth as he considered the warrior. He thought at first to complain as once again he felt he wasn't in control of his life, but thought better of it. Although deep inside he was disappointed Daniel wasn't here at this moment to guide him, he realized both the older man and the warrior saved his life several times now while putting their own lives in peril. He would trust both of the men since there was no immediate choice or reason not to.

Pushing with his feet, the seat twirled around, and Nolan was once again looking out the side window as the bullet raced along the monorail. From this vantage point he could see there were, what appeared to be, large floodlights spaced at regular intervals, lighting up the forest floor below them. However, upon closer inspection, he could see they weren't lights at all. They were a series of mirrors refracting light from the top of the 30-yard-thick platform to what would have otherwise been a dark, shadowed surface beneath the monumental structure.

Still facing the window, Nolan's words deflected back to Germaine. "Considering you're at war, aren't the pylons a major risk? I'd think, to your enemies, they'd be a prime target to bring down your city."

"Initially it would seem so, and you would think the risk would be re-doubled, considering only half the city is above the platform. The rest live and work within the cylindrical pylons with much of the industrial and commercial zones held within them. Our enemies, primarily the Toltec, understand this. Consequently, there have been several attacks through the ages, but not for quite some time. The key to defending a city is to know its weaknesses and those, when properly addressed, turn from a weakness to a strength." He pointed at the pylon just north of them as they passed it. "There are three protruding horizontal rings on the pylon. Do you see them?"

Nolan nodded. He saw one ring at the top of the pylon. One was near the surface, just above the vegetation, while the third ring was half-way between the other two.

"Each ring has four, 20-gigajoule phase cannons on them. Each gun is manned, running on a rail giving each of the powerful weapons a view over one quarter of the arc from the pylon. Considering the crossfire between pylons and the guns at three different levels, whether an attack was on foot, through the air or along the underside of the platform, it would be considered folly against such a defensive grid."

Nolan looked at the console momentarily. Six of the seven legs of their agenda were completed. Each time they switched to a different rail, the previous leg stopped flashing on the console and turned a solid green color.

Germaine continued the explanation of the defenses. "Only once has a pylon been brought down, and that was long ago. An air assault would have to somehow steal through the radar and anti-aircraft guns installed around the perimeter of the platform. On the ground, an attack would quickly be seen by the heat-seeking radar and the motion sensors. The phase cannons would make short work of anything that is identified."

"So how was the one pylon brought down?"

"Explosives. It was an inside job conducted by Toltec terrorists. Even then, only one pylon came down, and the platform held. With the strength of the structure along with the redundant engineering, it would take the destruction of at least three to compromise the integrity of the platform. That has never happened, and it never will," Germaine boasted.

Their bullet had been decelerating for a few minutes, and Nolan could see the rail in front of them was angling up into an opening in the platform. Slowing, but still at a speed of 60 miles an hour, the vehicle left the brightness of the refracted light, shooting up into the artificial light within the inner bowels of the city. The numeric sequence on the console had once again cued up. It read a 3 in the upper right corner. From that point in the arrival, the course of events happened in the reverse order to their departure. Once the cue went to zero, a crane took their bullet and moved it along the front of a massive parking structure—this one having five hundred stalls. The metal framework here was five stories high and the computer-controlled crane slid them into a stall on the fourth level. The grapple locked on the short section of slave-rail in the stall, jerking the bullet to a stop, the mechanical clang announcing the end of Nolan's first bullet ride. It took all of fifteen minutes.

Once again, the red light strobed across the bar at the top of the door, signaling it was about to open. Germaine motioned for Nolan to exit first. He complied and Germaine followed.

This station was much larger than the one underneath Daniel's lodging. There was also an elaborate terminal between the parking level and the ground level above. Bright, natural light showed through the curved glass arching over the terminal. The large glass panes let in the sunlight that now replaced the earlier rain, giving the terminal an atrium-like quality. The terminal was also bustling with people. They had already traveled up one escalator from the parking level, where Nolan could see a train of larger bullets through a window along the side of the terminal level. He assumed this was the Bailemor version of a subway. He also noticed, as they passed many stalls, that there were many sizes and shapes of personal bullets. He looked enviously at the sleek two-seaters and thought it humorous Germaine, warrior and leader of one hundred, had the station wagon of bullets.

They just stepped off the escalator bringing them to the surface level when they heard a commotion ahead. It didn't take them long to arrive within its midst, finding two men in each other's faces, bawling obscenities. From initial appearances it seemed likely one man had come up the escalator and bumped the other. Presently, finished with his tirade, he was bent over picking up the few papers strewn on the walkway.

Still mumbling under his breath, the man rose back to his feet, providing one last slur for the other man. "I should expect this type of clumsiness from an Akkadian!" he said, raising his voice once again.

Germaine stopped in his tracks, looking at the man as did several other men in the area. The man nervously reshuffled his papers in the folder and quickly turned, making a hasty departure up the roadway. None of the other men followed. The incident was over.

"Why did everyone get so uptight over a few freaking dropped papers?" Nolan questioned.

"It wasn't the papers. One man was an Akkadian, and the other was a Gwyneddman."

As they walked along the sidewalk, Nolan continued the line of questioning. "That's the second time I've heard the term 'Akkadian' and the first I've heard of a Gwyneddman. What are they?"

"There are two factions of people on Crann Bith and in the city of Bailemor. There are Akkadians and the Gwynedd. It has been so for hundreds of years. Everyone has an allegiance to one clan or the other, albeit some allegiances are loose. In many ways it's an outdated system, but it suffices to provide a loose government and a society having its interesting moments. For example, right now, an Akkadian leads the government, but his term is only five years, after which a Gwyneddman will rule in the cycle. There are also an equal number of councilors. Since it has been this way for many years, there's minimal quarreling or serious fighting over critical issues, and we move forward quickly."

"That seems an unusual, self-fulfilling twist to justify a system," Nolan stated. "How did you know one was an Akkadian and the other a Gwyneddman?"

"For a good observer, I'm surprised at your question. They wore their colors, and that was obvious."

Nolan smirked. "Humor me. I saw no colors."

Germaine stopped and pointed to his earring. It was a small silver button with a quarter-inch piece of royal-blue, polished stone housed within it. "They wore their earrings, which all in Bailemor wear. Blue is for the Akkadians; gold is for the Gwynedd."

Nolan took a second to inspect Germaine's blue stone. He turned his eyes to the street looking at the many travelers. Indeed, each had an earring he hadn't previously noticed. Most of the stones were blue while only a very few were gold. He turned back to Germaine who had continued walking. "There are many more Akkadians. I assume both Daniel and yourself are Akkadians?"

"Yes, we are. The breakdown of the two factions is almost equal, but for the most part we live apart. This platform on the west peak belongs to the Akkadians. The east peak you saw across the valley yesterday—that is for the Gwynedd."

"And what am I?"

Germaine chuckled. "You're what we call a heathen," he said with a wink. "But soon we hope you'll wear blue."

Nolan shuffled his feet to follow Germaine who was now walking up the steps of a long, wide, stone stairway fronting a large building. It had a stone façade, and cut into the stone were the words - *Skills Academy*. They strode across the top of the stairway, back down the steps on the other side, then onto a grass courtyard. They made their way across it, moving between numerous life-size statues.

"Who are they? Nolan asked.

"Heroes," Germaine replied with a sarcastic tone. "Most of these people died for Bailemor. They were great fighters through the ages, killers of our enemies and protectors of our people. Heroes—" he muttered "—dead, foolish heroes."

The rest of their walk was accomplished in silence until they arrived at a desk on the second floor of the west wing of the complex. Here, Germaine handed a piece of paper to a uniformed man sitting at a desk, showed him his security clearance, then turned back to face Nolan. "You have a survey to fill out before you meet an advisor. I'll be back here in two hours to fetch you." With that, Germaine turned on his heels before his quick steps took him back from the direction he had come.

The uniformed man asked Nolan to follow him further into the depths of the building and through several large wooden doors into a smaller, austere office occupied by a frail looking man barely large enough to fill the uniform he wore.

Germaine had not led Nolan astray. There indeed was a survey with the man asking him ten pages of questions. Everything from his physical history and illnesses to his skills and abilities, were queried. The man showed a piqued interest when Nolan explained his flying skills. The survey was tedious, but Nolan learned as much about the Academy from the line of questions as the advisor learned about him. Finally, the frail man slapped his book closed with a surprisingly strong motion of his hand, signaling the interview was over. As if on cue, the first uniformed man entered the room to lead Nolan away.

Once again, he was being led down a long hallway and through several doors. Nolan asked, "Where are we going?"

Without turning his eyes, the soldier said, "We are going to see Captain Welland. Every new recruit coming from off-world needs an accelerated program. That means a tutor. Captain Welland has been assigned to you."

Great, Nolan thought. *All I need is a kick-ass, cigar smoking, fat-lipped, and even fatter-assed captain to ride my butt.* He rolled his eyes as the soldier opened a door, motioning him to enter.

A large wooden desk was the focal point of the room. On the far side was a wide, black, leather chair with a coat draped over the back. On the near side of the desk were two smaller chairs, and one was occupied. Nolan sat in the vacant one, peeking sideways at the occupant of the other chair. He slowly raised his eyes to him, verifying they had not deceived him. Sitting beside Nolan was a well-built, somewhat sloppy looking man. However, it was his hair that shocked Nolan. It was cropped short at the top, longer at the back and was a bright-blue color.

With blue still on his mind from earlier in the day, Nolan said with a smile, "You must be Akkadian."

The blue-haired man looked at Nolan quizzically, but did not respond.

Nolan made a second effort, pointing to the man's head. "Your hair—it's blue."

The man, who could not be older than 25 in Nolan's estimation, leaned forward, his black, piercing eyes returning Nolan's stare. "On my world all the people have colored hair—bright red, green or blue. Blue is a noble color. Only criminals and those afflicted with disease or poverty don't color their hair." As he spoke the words, he glanced up at Nolan's plain, brown hair.

For a few seconds, Nolan was at a loss for words, but he liked the steady, firm voice from the man. He pushed out his hand. "My name is Nolan."

A hesitant smile crossed the other man's face. After a few seconds, he swung his hand out, clasping Nolan's. "I'm Lukas."

At that moment, there was a crack behind them, as the door was opened. *Freaking hell,* Nolan thought. *Here comes the fat-ass captain.*

The two men unclasped their hands while keeping their eyes forward, burning a hole into the back of the chair opposite them.

The footsteps were lighter than Nolan expected. A fragrance came to his nose—*lavender,* he thought, trying to bring back the memory from his suddenly confused mind. He lifted his eyes to the right, and his fingers tightened on the wooden arms of the chair. The steps continued around him as the captain slid into the high-backed chair.

Nolan struggled to keep his mouth from dropping. The captain wore civilian clothes, and they were tight-fitting. The thought kept repeating over and over in his mind as his gaze locked on her. The fat-assed captain was in fact not fat-assed, although his attention there was only momentary, as it was drawn more so by the way her breasts filled the thin sweater. She also had shoulder-length, red hair with a slight curl at the base of her slender neck. It complimented her green, cat-like eyes.

As Nolan sat speechless, Lukas was the first to address her. "You really think you should be sitting in the captain's chair?"

Nolan's tight smile held back the laughter as his cheeks slightly bulged. He appreciated his father's guidance, preaching caution when approaching the unknown. His eyes stayed on her, thinking the woman's features became even more attractive even as her cheeks flushed with a hint of anger.

She leaned forward, putting both arms on the desk, intertwining her fingers. "I *am* the captain," the woman said, looking from one man to the other. "Captain Deahna Welland. I'm a civilian on contract to the Academy. It seems, through their research and many years of experience, the Academy has come to the conclusion hard-nosed captains who are veterans of the service and consider their yelling tone to be acceptable for normal conversation, aren't the optimal fit for a virginal cadet who has just come into the greater world of the Athar."

Nolan took a peek at Lukas who carried a sly smile on his face, then turned his eyes back to the captain. The color of her cheeks returned to normal, but he still had difficulty keeping his eyes from her. Her eyes sparkled with life, and her thin lips, painted pink, framed a sarcastic smile. Notwithstanding, it lit up her face.

Through the smile, she continued her introduction. "I would be just as happy being a civilian worker. Even as it is, I keep things informal. Both of you can call me Deahna. I really didn't want to be called *captain* or hold the rank, but after the incident with Cadet Koren, 18 months ago, the senior officials thought it better I hold an official rank."

Lukas jumped in feet first. "What happened with Cadet Koren?"

She shifted herself in the chair, closer to Lukas, her voice soft with a touch of sweetness. "He was assigned to me, but he saw himself with an excess of testosterone, and he saw me as a simple civilian. Even more so, he thought of me as a weak woman."

Lukas leaned forward with his sly grin growing, "So what did the weak woman do?"

Leaning an elbow on the table, Deahna put her chin on her palm, her fingers strumming against her jaw. Her face was tilted to the side, her voice maintaining the soft sound of innocence. "He pushed my button too far one day. I twisted his arm behind him and pressed him hard into the wall right behind you." She pointed to a spot left of the door opening. "The blood made quite a mess of the carpet, but then the amount of blood is relative to how badly a nose is broken. Considering the look of his post-impact nose, I considered the carpet replacement as an acceptable collateral loss." Her sweet smile widened.

Lukas snapped back in his chair. "I understand."

Nolan looked over at Lukas, thinking, *if he had a tail, it would be between his legs right now.*

"Unfortunately, the senior ranks didn't see it so simply," Deahna said. "They didn't mind an arrogant cadet getting his chops busted, but it looked bad if it was a civilian who did the busting. To avoid a repeat of the problem, they made me a captain, but that's in the past—right? Let's get back to the matter at hand. A tutor is assigned to every two new off-world cadets. Your introduction to this world needs to be accelerated, and there is much for you to know. I'll be spending quite a bit of time with each of you."

That was the last thing Nolan paid attention to. The rest of the woman's words sounded like a sweet song playing in the background as the words he wanted to hear kept repeating in his mind. She had said, "I will spend quite a bit of time with each of you."

It had been some time since Nolan had been with a woman. This woman had spirit, and she was a beauty. He was drawn, wanting to know more about her. Hearing her sweet voice explaining what he needed to know was what he wanted, but he couldn't help but think, *what he needed to know was all about her.* Taking the time to engrain her vision into his memory, his eyes scanned over her form. He didn't want to move his focus from her perfectly formed face, but eventually his inspection panned down her body. He frowned for a moment, finding the desk partially obscured her, but it was short-lived when he saw her long slim legs under the bottom edge of it. At the end of the shapely legs were two well-proportioned feet with painted toes, and she wore open-toed high heels. Nolan had a smug look on his face, as he thought, *Germaine would be more than satisfied.*

Chapter 3

The all-terrain vehicle bounced across the salt flat. It was dusk and the best time to draw very little attention to the six-wheeled vehicle. Julian, holding the steering wheel with one hand, could still see in the waning light. The headlights that might draw attention to his movements, were not yet needed.

He was making good time, having left the highway between the city of Kaezzar and Lake Fuego, five minutes ago. The short drive across the salt-flat had been uneventful, but now he was crossing the area bounding the path of the overhead water and power supply lines. Here, the ground was much more irregular. Thankfully, he saw the flattened tracks ahead, recognizing it as the rarely used service road paralleling the line of steel towers supporting the supply lines. He turned onto it, heading north toward his destination. Thankfully, the throbbing in his arm lessened with the reduced undulations in the surface now travelled.

He cursed under his breath: first at Nolan Harrison, then at Daniel Dupuis and finally at the damn beast having torn open his arm with its sharp fangs. He flexed his fingers. It had only been a few days since the attack and his subsequent return to Kaezzar. The pain was now more bearable, but he still seethed at the sequence of events. The doctors, not knowing the origin of the attacking beast, nor the diseases it could carry, gave Julian the full complement of precautionary medical shots in what seemed to him every vulnerable part of his body. *His ass hurt almost as much as his arm,* he thought while continuing the curses.

And for all his efforts and suffering, there was nothing to show for it but his heavily bandaged arm. Nolan, Daniel and the third Celtae, in all likelihood, escaped to Bailemor, but the Celtae had much to reconsider if they thought Julian Morenz gave up so easily. If anything, his resolve was heightened, and his fixation with Nolan's capture had truly turned into an obsession.

He peered out the windshield of the open-wheeled vehicle, watching the tower numbers flash by as he passed each steel structure. Seeing the sign -

Tower 382, he braked hard. The vehicle screeched to a halt, throwing up a billowing salt cloud. Julian threw the shift lever in reverse, then parked the vehicle next to the steel girders on the far side of the tower. He looked at his watch, seeing he was still 15 minutes early.

The sun continued its downward path behind the horizon. The normally yellow sky now included wisps of purple, as the light reflected off the intermittent clouds. Under the calm sky, Julian kicked open the door of the vehicle, sliding his short frame down until his boots hit the dirt. Small dust clouds pressed up into the air. He glanced frequently at his watch, and in between his glances, which became more frustrated as each minute went by, he nervously tapped the side of the vehicle with his fingers. He was waiting for someone.

By now, the purple runners had left the horizon, and the darkness of a cold Kaezzar night set in. Only the meager reflected light from the stars in the sky kept Julian from a feeling of total panic. He felt uncomfortable with the vulnerability of being isolated here in the barren flats.

Julian almost jumped out of his skin when he heard the movement right beside him. Not a yard away, leaning against the vehicle, was a tall, cloaked figure. The sound that had shattered the silence was only the cracking of a match, as the figure lit a pipe that ended somewhere in the shadow of the hood over his head.

Julian shifted a step away from the dark man as he said, "You're late."

The shadowy figure hadn't yet looked at Julian. "In my business schedules and deadlines are secondary to the result of the exploits," he said quietly. He inhaled on the pipe as the brief amber glow revealed a cold face with piercing eyes and a sharp, clean-shaven chin.

Julian needed to be careful. The man was a spy and an assassin—a killer for hire, if need be, who likely would kill him as easily as take his contract if he felt it suited him. He cleared his throat. "I understand you have spent time in Bailemor."

The man's face turned to Julian. "I understand you have work you require completed in Bailemor." His words came in a slow drawl.

Julian handed over the large envelope. "Daniel Dupuis is a native of Bailemor. He's a veteran of the Watch, highly decorated and now retired. Nolan Harrison is from a plane called Earth, and Mr. Dupuis went to quite a bit of effort to bring him to Bailemor. For some reason, he feels the Earthman is special. I need to know why."

The shadowed figure pulled each picture and profile from the envelope. His eyes engrained the information into his memory. He reached further down into the envelope, pulling out a small credit card with the number *10,000* printed across the top. "This is only half the fee," he questioned, his lowered eyebrow a sinister addition to his already menacing countenance.

"The other half will come when I receive the information on Nolan Harrison."

There was a large scar along the length of the spy's hand, becoming visible as he pressed the pictures and dossiers back into the envelope. He raised the corner of the envelope to his pipe and inhaled deeply several times. Finally, the corner lit in flame, and soon the orange flicker grew to consume the entire portfolio, except the corner held within the tips of his fingers. He dropped it, letting the flames die out, leaving the contents nothing but black ashes. "Agreed," he whispered. "We have a contract. Would you like me to use any prudence regarding my behavior in the accomplishment of the task?"

Julian replied icily. "I don't want Harrison killed. As for the rest of your methods, I wouldn't want to limit your creativity." He laughed at his own attempted humor and slapped his hand in triumph against the side of the vehicle. The laugh turned to a howl, as he had inadvertently struck his damaged arm against the steel. In only a few seconds, he recovered, shaking his hand as he looked up to the spy, but he was gone. Julian spun on his toe, searching in all directions, but there was no sign of the dark figure. All that remained was the slightly acrid odor from the combination of burnt herbs from the man's pipe.

Julian rubbed his thin beard. He was curious about the man who very few had ever seen face to face. The name he was known by was Peron, and he had come highly recommended by the best references, so he assumed he would hear from him soon enough.

Still having another appointment to attend to, Julian seated himself back in the all-terrain vehicle. He carefully drove up the service road a few hundred yards before turning the lights on. Several small, red lizards scampered out of the sudden, bright onslaught. He paid them no attention as he turned the wheel, making a bee-line for the highway. From the point he turned back on the highway, he drove east for 30 minutes until the sign - *Bolivar Station Steam Division*, signified he had reached his second destination.

Julian drove the all-terrain vehicle into the garage of the complex after the steel plate door opened, triggered by the magnetic strip embedded in the driveway. Another strip inside the garage monitored his vehicle's progress, and the door swung shut behind him. A second containment door opened after the first was secured. He pressed the gas pedal and as the car passed the second door, a photo eye was triggered, allowing this door to close. Thankfully, the temperature in this part of the complex was controlled at 80 degrees. Although warmer than the average temperature in the city, it was much more comfortable than the 110-degree temperatures outside at the base of Lake Fuego.

A security guard came forth from the small room situated adjacent to the driveway just in front of the security barrier. The commander showed him his security card and divulged his appointment with the warden. The guard raised his hand, pointing to the parking spots alongside the wall visible across the other side of the parking level. With a hand signal from the first guard, a second guard in the security room pressed a button, and the barrier tilted upward, allowing Julian's continued progress into the complex.

Warden Biels met him halfway down the main corridor from the parking level to the office complex. The temperature here was a much more pleasant 70 airconditioned degrees. Julian evaluated the warden as he came closer. The smile on the warden's face couldn't mask his furtive eyes darting nervously back and forth. Julian knew already, even before an introduction, he could control this man.

"Commander Morenz, welcome to Bolivar," Warden Biels said.

Julian gave the warden a sympathetic smile. "It's good to be here. I hope the repairs from the attack are progressing well?"

"Very well, in fact. The perimeter walls were repaired within 48 hours of the attack, and the damaged generators were operational another 48 hours after that. Now, we are just doing final aesthetic touch-ups," Warden Biels replied.

"That's impressive, especially considering the workers at this facility are criminals, for the most part," Julian said in an insincere, pacifying tone.

Putting a hand on Julian's shoulder, the warden said, "Since this is a rehabilitation facility, we don't call them criminals or convicts. They are *associates*." He smiled. "Just, for some, the association has a longer term. This would be the case for Associate Tulis. He is the one you have an interest in." His hand slid off Julian's shoulder and reached for the folder tucked securely under his arm. He handed it to the commander.

Julian's eyes widened as he felt the warden's hand on his shoulder since it was the one attached to his bandaged arm. He silently forgave the warden's indiscretion, seeing him hand over the folder which was the reason he was here.

Warden Biels took a backward sidestep, and his hand pointed down the hall. "Associate Tulis is working in Generator room 15. You can see him there."

Without hesitation and comfortable being in the lead, Julian stepped down the hallway, hearing the warden's footsteps close behind. He opened the folder and immediately thought he was looking at a picture of Adrian Korlis. *He already found what he came here to confirm,* he thought with a chuckle. Indeed, it was clear Jelan Tulis was the brother of Adrian Korlis. Upon closer inspection, he could see Jelan was a few years younger and a little thinner, but the shape of face and the strong eyes easily matched him to the man who was Julian's superior.

There was very little written information in the folder. Basic identifying marks, age, height and weight were the only items noted. There was a location on the form to indicate the reason for his incarceration. On this line the word – *Classified,* was typed. There was also a required field for length of incarceration, and on this line was the word - *Indefinite.* Julian turned his head to the side. "It doesn't say why he is here or for how long."

"It means he's here at the request of the government. That's all we know other than not to ask questions. As for his length of stay, there have been some state prisoners who have died here. For others, they stay until one day, unannounced, state officials show up with the requisite paperwork, and the prisoner is whisked away. For what purpose, I don't know, and I don't ask," Warden Biels said with a shrug.

Julian had a smug smile on his face. "That's very commendable. I'll be sure to notify the senator in charge of penal systems of the wonderful job you're doing here."

Not recognizing the sarcasm in Julian's voice, the warden's face lit up. He pointed to a side door off the hallway. "We are here." He propped open the door with his arm, letting Julian pass through into Generator room 15.

The generator room was large and two floors high. Julian found himself on a catwalk running around the entire perimeter of the second floor of the room. The large, whining electrical device was centrally located with five men working around it. Two of the men, clipboards in their hands, were monitoring instruments on the generator. They were more fortunate than the other three who had been given a work detail. A small office was in the midst of construction in the corner of the room. Supplies had come in, and the three men were moving them from the roll-up door where they had been received, to the other side of the room where the office was being erected. Unfortunately for the three, all that was left were the thin steel beams that would make up the corners and studs for the frame, packaged in sets of five. Two of the men, with one at each end of the eight-foot-long packet, lifted, shimmying the weight across the room.

Julian recognized the third man as Jelan Tulis even though he had several days growth of stubble on his face. His shirt was pulled off, leaving him to work only in the white, tank-top undershirt that was part of the standard uniform. *The man is huge,* Julian thought. He definitely was Adrian's brother, based on the facial features, but Jelan was obviously more youthful. In fact, he was quite a few years younger than Adrian, with a very strong, muscular physique. Amazingly, he was carrying the load of metal studs singularly, keeping up with the other two men who worked together. As he lifted, his left bicep flexed, molding the skin into flowing curves as the muscles underneath stretched them into an aggressive shape. Around the muscle was a band of blue.

Julian turned from his position leaning against the railing to face Warden Biels. "What's the blue band on his arm?"

"It's not a band. It's a tattoo that circles the muscle. Here in the station, many of the associates make tattooing a hobby. Funny though, he had the tattoo before he came here," he mumbled while lost in thought. After a few seconds, he saw the frustrated look in Julian's eyes. "Perhaps you would like to go down and meet him and review it more closely."

"No, I'm finished here." Julian made determined steps out the door, retracing his steps back the way he had come. He was deep in thought. *The issue of Nolan Harrison was not going well, but at least Jelan Tulis's identity was confirmed. It would be an effective weapon in his arsenal, available for leverage against Adrian Korlis when the need came.* The thought left him with a satisfied smile on his face.

The smile might well have vanished if he had taken the time to be more thorough. It is true that it's the details and putting in that extra effort that makes people successful. He might not have recognized it right away, but in time, he would have noticed, if he had gone down to see Jelan Tulis face to face. The blue tattoo was really a mosaic pattern of intermingled curved lines, resembling the appearance of an ancient carved stone castle wall. The tattoo was intricate with five individual coins drawn within the band at regular intervals around the arm. If Julian had taken the time to look, he would have seen the round shapes were not really coins, but made to look so. Each was actually a round ring surrounding a familiar pattern—that of a crossed hammer and sword.

Chapter 4

Looking out from the patio of Daniel's home, Nolan admired the afternoon view of Bailemor. Directly in front was the Akkadian mountain spiraling up through the Upper City. Swiveling his head to the right, he could see the second mountain tip referred to simply as the Summit. Thinner but higher than the other two peaks, it was reserved exclusively for government offices and residences of the highest-ranking officials. As such, he considered the Summit appropriately named.

Nolan, sitting back in a colorful blue and yellow cushioned chair, shifted his feet and crossed his ankles, resting them on the small table in front of himself. Behind him, out of his view, was the third peak of Bailemor occupied primarily by the Gwynedd faction. He found the story of Gwyneddmen and Akkadians interesting. At first, he thought it silly and similar to gangs on Earth, wearing their colors, but as Germaine explained, it made sense.

The warrior had frowned when Nolan referred to the two factions as gangs. Germaine explained there were many things in life that were unavoidable. Rather than spending exorbitant amounts of futile energy and resources trying to curb the activities, why not work with the vice, and guide it to a better purpose? As such, the so-called gangs were not only tolerated, but promoted. With structured guidance, the traits of teamwork, trust and honor were the lifeblood of the Akkadians and the Gwyneddmen. The younger men and women weren't allowed to wear their colorful earrings until their eighteenth birthday. This avoided most of the violent conflicts a young spirit brings, but not all. There were still some outbreaks of violence, Germaine had explained, but they were much less frequent than what would have occurred if outright abolition had been adopted. Nolan considered the argument from Germaine compelling.

Nolan didn't hear the door open. The sun was square in his eyes, reflecting off the plate glass doors behind him, then reflected a second time back against the flower box in front of him, indicating the door had been shifted. Someone was there. He picked up his orange-colored fruit drink, pulling it to his lips as he waited for the person to speak.

"Hello, Nolan." The familiar voice of Daniel glided down to the younger man.

Nolan's head snapped around with a wide smile. "It's about time you showed up. I've missed you." His words were sincere. It had been five days since Nolan's arrival on Crann Bith. Although he was concerned Daniel had left him as soon as he arrived, the heart-felt, honest friendship he held with the older man shone through the shadow of doubt.

Daniel lowered himself into the chair next to Nolan. Outwardly, the weathered appearance was lost. His hair was neatly trimmed as was his moustache. The faded clothes were gone, now replaced by an expensive looking outfit. The jacket and slacks were both of a dark, copper-colored material which matched well with the loose-fitting, black shirt. Highlighting his appearance was the blue-stoned earring sparkling in his right ear lobe. "Unfortunately, there was some urgent business to attend to as soon as we arrived," he offered apologetically.

"Hopefully it doesn't always take you this long to get cleaned up," Nolan said as he chuckled.

The mirroring laugh coming from Daniel's lips was as much from relief as the reaction to the humorous comment. "I left you in very capable hands. I trust Germaine with my life, so it is obvious I would trust him with yours." The jovial facade didn't reveal Daniel's feelings of guilt, leaving as he did, but it had been very necessary. He was thankful and quite impressed with Nolan's reaction. The Earth man had changed in the short time he had known him. He didn't make poorly guided assumptions, and he showed the patience to let events play out before jumping to conclusions. Daniel kept these thoughts to himself, including the hope that the younger man was indeed the First Key, but more than that was the basic hope that he would continue to learn and grow.

There were a few moments of silence as they watched the sun move lower on the horizon. It was finally broken by Daniel. "How are things at the Skills Academy?"

Nolan's face brightened as the question instinctively brought the vision of Deahna into his mind. He saw her over and over in his thoughts and dreams since they had met, and he hadn't felt like this for a very long time. It was silly, not knowing the woman well yet feeling a very strong connection.

Nolan's daydream was broken by the smack of Daniel's hand on his shoulder. "Nolan?"

Pulled from his fantasy, the younger man's gray eyes turned to Daniel. "Everything is set. In four days, I begin my term. I've been told I'll be staying there for four days, then allowed out for three. The schedule will continue until I've graduated."

"Who is your partner?"

"A man named Lukas. We've already spent a little time together. He seems a good man, and he has pride that will make him a good mate. The two of us are teamed up with six others assigned to Squad 33." He turned his head nonchalantly away from Daniel. "Captain Deahna Welland is the tutor for both Lukas and I."

"You have made excellent strides since I have been gone."

Nolan's fingers rolled along the rim of his glass. "Where did you go?"

Daniel's sigh told Nolan it wasn't an altogether pleasant trip for the older man. "I went to visit my bond brother."

"I haven't heard the term 'bond brother' before."

Daniel was lost in thought for a few seconds before he responded. "Our population on Crann Bith is not healthy. Right now, it is a little over five hundred thousand inhabitants. Fifty years ago, our population was eight hundred thousand. You can see the war takes its toll as it has for centuries. With that in mind, there are many men and women who were mothers and fathers, who died. Consequently, there have been many children who, although not abandoned, have been very much alone without a caring ear for their thoughts, or to hear their hopes and aspirations."

Nolan listened. He knew well enough the tone Daniel was speaking in. This was important to him.

"So, many years ago, the citizens of Bailemor developed an alternative. When a child turns ten, his parents make an arrangement with another family for the two children to be bonded. The two boys are not told the name of the other until they are 16. This is to maintain the confidentiality of trust which is considered very sacred to the people of Crann Bith. The bond brother is someone the man knows he can confide in with the utmost trust. It is unheard of for a bond brother to be revealed. The secrecy of the relationship is what allows the discussions and sharing of feelings between the two to be so open and honest. It has helped our race in this time of war. There are many young men growing up without the guidance of parents who benefit from having a bond brother."

Nolan knew not to ask who Daniel's bond brother was, but the words did make him think. His parents weren't here. If something happened to Germaine or especially Daniel, he would be very much alone in this world. Turning again to look at the older man, Nolan said, "I have some other questions."

Daniel chuckled. "Of course. Some things do not change."

Nolan gave Daniel a friendly scowl. "Our escape from Earth was interesting. One of the Toltec helped you."

"Yes, it seems he was instrumental," Daniel replied.

Nolan lowered an eyebrow. "Don't you find that odd—a Toltec, and sworn enemy of the Celtae for centuries, helping a Celtae prisoner escape?"

"Now that you mention it, it *was* unusual. The Toltec was a nice fellow," Daniel generously offered, a playful smile on his lips.

"Okay, cut the freaking crap! I saw the same tattoo on both your chest and on the Toltec who helped us. What is it that I need to know?"

Through the grin Daniel said, "Very well. The tattoo has a meaning, but it is something better understood if I show you rather than tell you."

"Very well." Nolan waved an arm in frustration before crossing his arms on his chest. "Don't let me hold you back."

"Not now," Daniel said. "Tomorrow we are going on a field trip to another plane. There, you will learn all there is to know. Until then, be patient."

Nolan opened his mouth to protest, but Daniel had already risen and was moving back into the depth of the apartment. The discussion was over.

The next day began with the sound of a sharp rap on the door to Nolan's room. Nolan pried his eyes open with several aggressive blinks. He looked to the window and saw nothing but the pitch-black of night. Hearing the rap repeated, he turned his head and acknowledged with a hoarse voice through his sleepiness, "I'm up!"

Nolan heard the footfalls become softer as the perpetrator who interrupted his slumber, moved down the hallway. Giving his head a shake, he quickly moved to the bathroom and went through the same ritualistic motions—relieving his bladder, shaving, then a quick shower with the temperature of the water just under the scalding point. Usually, he changed before he went into the living area of Daniel's home, but he didn't know what clothing would be appropriate for the field trip mentioned the day before. Consequently, he pulled his sleeping clothes back on with a thin housecoat providing a final layer.

In the dining area, just off the kitchen, he found both Germaine and Daniel casually dressed. They were eating the round, sweet buns which constituted breakfast for most Bailemorians. Pulling out the chair he laid claim to these last few days, he sat down as his eyes searched through the basket of buns. His fingers slid forward, pulling out the bun he sought—the one having a flavor similar to cinnamon.

Nolan watched the two men, paying particular attention to Daniel. He rolled his eyes as he saw the now familiar eating mode the older man employed. The edge of the bun was eaten all the way around in a neat circle. Germaine utilized a more conventional approach with his large bites cutting halfway across the sweet bun held within his fingers.

Between hungry bites of the sweet bun, Nolan said, "It's awful early in the morning."

Pulling his arm in front of him, Daniel glimpsed his watch. "Yes, in fact, it is 3:00 in the morning."

Nolan continued to eat the bun as his eyes conveyed a message to both of the men. He wasn't impressed.

Daniel stretched his arms over his head, yawning. "The field trip is more of a mission, and you can come along to help. It will give you some experience with another planer hop, and along the way, the mysterious tattoos you questioned will be explained." With that, Daniel rose to his feet, stating, "Let's go."

Daniel led the way through the hallway to the bedrooms, and at the back of the hallway was a locked door that Nolan always assumed was a closet of some sort. Daniel quickly unlocked the door, pulling it open on well-oiled hinges, revealing a steep, long set of stairs. Nolan lifted himself up on his tip toes as he spied the landing below and another set of stairs continuing the downward zigzag of steps. Germaine led the way. Nolan was in the middle while Daniel brought up the rear after he locked the door. Their descent continued along three flights of steps until their progress was halted by another door. This one was sturdy, made of reinforced steel with a heavy dead-bolt lock. This door was also unlocked and pulled open. Daniel popped his head out, peering in one direction, then the other. After the quick inspection, he waved his hand, indicating the coast was clear to continue.

The three men shuffled through the doorway. Through the dim, artificial light, Nolan saw they were in a service corridor deep in the bowels of the platform. The Earthman began his protest. "I'm not dressed for this…"

Daniel was already in his mission mode, and he interrupted the younger man's words. "You will get clothes and everything else you need in a moment."

The service corridor was two stories high and curved off endlessly in both directions. Along each side of the tunnel-shaped passageway were two catwalks running the length of the shaft with one just above the other. At intervals of every one hundred yards was a bowed, catwalk-style bridge, crossing from one upper catwalk to the catwalk on the other side of the tunnel. It was along the narrow upper catwalk where the three men now walked toward the far catwalk bridge just ahead of them. As they crossed, Nolan saw the monorail above them. He realized this tunnel must be reserved for bullet service vehicles.

Once on the other side, Daniel led the way toward one of many doors dotting both sides of the tunnel. With the same key he used on the previous steel door, he unlocked this door and shuffled inside. Nolan and Germaine followed, and the door swung shut with a clang echoing down the length of the tunnel. They were in total darkness. Nolan dared not move.

Nolan heard a small click followed by a slight electrical discharge, and the room was illuminated by six overhead, incandescent lights. The three of them were standing in a large storeroom—30 feet long by 25 feet wide. In the center of the room was a large, black square painted on the floor. Around it, dotting the gray walls, were numerous objects. Hanging from one wall of Daniel's personal storeroom was almost every type of weapon one could imagine. There were different types of rifles and pistols, and alongside them was an armory of swords, shields, knives and bows. There were also many hand-to-hand weapons which were unfamiliar to Nolan, and he thought it just as well, considering the ruthless killing potential he saw in them.

Walking to the wall of weapons, Daniel pulled down a large sheathed knife and tossed it to Nolan. Two more similar knives and two curved swords, sheathed in scabbards, were also pulled off their hangers. Then Daniel made his way to a series of short cupboards mounted at knee-level on the opposite wall. Above them, hung on a rail, were numerous pieces of clothing covering the wall from one end to the other. Handing the weapons to Germaine as he walked by him, Daniel moved to the far corner of the room, curling a finger behind him, motioning the two men to follow. Daniel slid the hangers back and forth a few times before he pulled down three of them. Each held an outfit of cold-weather gear.

Nolan took one of the outfits from Daniel's offering hand. "I take it we're not going to the beach?" he said, sarcastically.

Daniel began to strip out of his clothes as he responded. "That we are not, my friend. It is cold on the Toltec world we are going to, and it could be dangerous." He nodded toward the weapons.

Watching the other two men dress, Nolan mimicked their actions. He disrobed down to his undergarments and pulled on a long-sleeved, thin t-shirt. Although it was light, he could feel it was made of an unusual, packed material with a good insulation value. There were a similar pair of inner pants he also pulled on. The bottoms, covered with long, thick socks, were made to hug his feet. Next, he stepped into the thick trousers made of white fur. A parka made of a similar material was pulled overhead, leaving the hood to hang down over the back of his neck.

Daniel pulled out thick boots for the three of them. Nolan slipped his feet into his, pulling the velcro strap at the top, tight. With some reservation, he secured the belt at his waist and slid the large knife into the loop attached at the side. Wrapping the scarf over the lower half of his face and pulling on the warm gloves, he looked similar to Germaine and Daniel, except they each had an extra belt over their shoulder where the sword hung across their backs. The last thing the older man pressed into an inner pocket was a pair of binoculars.

Daniel led them to the middle of the black square on the floor and placed his hand on Nolan's shoulder. "The hop could leave you dizzy, and it will be cold when we get there. Hold on."

Nolan gripped Daniel's forearm with both hands.

Lifting his other hand, Daniel placed the scarf over his mouth and nose, then gripped Germaine's shoulder.

Closing his eyes, Nolan invoked the Athar to his mind's eye. It came clearly, and he saw the pulse of the one marker Daniel had lit up for him. He focused on the brightness, willing himself there, and it was only a moment later when he felt the butterflies in his stomach and the feeling of falling.

Nolan's hands slipped as he felt the dizziness come over him. Before he recovered, a blast of frigid air assaulted him, pushing him several stumbling steps backward through the pelting snow.

Both Germaine and Daniel grabbed one of Nolan's arms to keep him from losing his feet altogether. Daniel pressed his face close to Nolan's. His eyes, barely open to slits, bored into the younger man's as they were pummeled by the strong wind laden with ice particles. There was no use trying to talk through the scarf or over the howl of the wind. Daniel's eyes were questioning as he raised a gloved hand, the thumb pointed upward. Nolan shifted his feet, steadying himself as he nodded his head up and down. He raised his own fist, the thumb pointed upward. He had just successfully completed his second planer hop.

Daniel's eyes smiled while his hand gripped the thick coat at Nolan's shoulder, giving it a reassuring shake. Then, he pointed through the darkness of the night toward a line of barely visible trees in the distance. The three men stayed close together, walking briskly across the flat, open field toward the tree line, and after ten minutes, they were thankful to reach their protection. They kept moving as the snow-covered forest of long-needled trees grew thicker. Another ten minutes went by, and the howl of the wind was gone, as was the chill in their bones.

Daniel pulled down his scarf, revealing his moustache covered in ice. His words came in a shroud of condensed vapor. "The cold is bearable here, so you can remove your scarves."

Nolan complied and actually found the temperature in the forest quite comfortable. The layer of air between the inner lining of clothes and the fur outerwear, provided excellent insulating qualities. The scene was also peaceful. Each tree had a wide array of branches coated in needles sparkling blue-green in the star light that traversed through the cloudless sky. Each branch supported a layer of snow, causing them to slouch downward, allowing the lower ones to brush the carpet of snow blanketing the ground.

Daniel pointed through the forest while again placing his other hand on Nolan's shoulder. "We are going to a small village about half a mile in that direction." He looked at Germaine. "Hang back 50 yards. Cover our rear."

Germaine nodded in silence, then his even quieter footfalls carried him off into the woods.

The two men, side by side, walked through the trees. After a short time, their legs began to ache, as the snow was eight inches deep. The run of the land was flat until they came upon a gradual downward slope. Here, Daniel raised his arm, indicating a stop, before he lowered to one knee within the branches of a fallen tree. Nolan slid to one knee beside him. Daniel brought the binoculars from his pocket, then up to his eyes as his head panned slowly from side to side. As he peered through the light snow that had just begun to fall, his head stopped, and his finger came around the side of the lens to adjust the focus. He took a good five minutes looking through the binoculars during which time Germaine had come from the rear to join them. Without moving his eyes from his interest in the distance, Daniel flipped his hand, passing the binoculars to Nolan.

Pressing back the hood of his fur parka, Nolan brought the binoculars up to his eyes and looked into the distance, following Daniel's line of sight. He saw a small clearing with six small structures surrounded by the forest. There were lights on in three of the buildings, but then he revaluated. It must be fire or lantern light, based on the flickering. Bringing the binoculars forward, he frowned. He just realized it was very dark, yet he could see clearly through the binoculars for a distance of three hundred yards.

Daniel turned his head. "They have some unique enhancements you might not have seen before."

Nolan brought the eyepieces back up and continued to survey the settlement.

"You see the village," Daniel verified.

"Yes."

"On the left, there is a building without lights. Look carefully. There is a guard in the shadow of the porch."

"I see him," Nolan replied.

"Do you see any other people?"

Nolan panned the village for several more seconds. "No, just the one person."

Daniel held out his hand and Nolan returned the binoculars. In a squat, he turned on his toes, facing Germaine and Nolan. "This is a Toltec-held world and peaceful for the most part. The Celtae have left them alone because these people live in history. They do not have electricity or any type of energy-based operations. They are religious, believing in a simple life, serving their god. It is unfortunate that, from time to time, someone will stray from that doctrine, and this is the case now. Inside the dark building, an energy source is being secretly developed. Toltecs from another plane have hidden it here, and we are here to take photographs of the plans and destroy it."

Nolan nodded and asked, "How?"

"The people are passive. They will not be a problem except for the big fellow guarding the building. I suspect he is from the plane that developed the energy source. He needs to be dispatched." Daniel's eyes, steel blue in the starlight, bored into Nolan.

"What do you mean—dispatched?"

"Dispatched—terminated—killed."

"This can't be done without loss of life?" Nolan queried. The words came slowly off his tongue.

"I do not see another way," Daniel responded. "Germaine and I will move closer from this direction. You will make a wide arc around the settlement, and come at the building from the other side. After you have dispatched the stranger, signal us, and we will join you inside."

Nolan's eyes opened wide. "I'm not killing him!" he said through clenched teeth.

"You are one of us now, and you are part of this war. They are Toltec, and in a war, there are casualties. You need to do your part," Daniel urged.

Nolan slammed his fist into his palm as his eyes burned into Daniel. "I'm not killing anyone here! These people have done nothing to me. They're innocent and passive. I really don't care about your freaking Akkadian ways, and if this is what you people do, then I don't want any part of your war!"

"Are you sure?"

"Very freaking sure!" Nolan blurted.

Daniel said, "There is a war going on and…"

"I'm not a cold-blooded killer!"

Daniel looked at Germaine, then a wry smile came across his lips as he turned back to Nolan. "That is good."

"Huh?" Nolan had a confused look on his face.

Daniel put his hand on Nolan's shoulder, pulling him closer. "We did not have any intention of killing anyone. There are things you need to know about Germaine and I—things that would put us in great peril if you were an aggressive sort who would thrive in this damn war."

Nolan's eyes began to burn with anger.

Daniel's words squashed the look before it had fully developed. "Understand, our lives and the lives of many others were at stake. The knowledge you will gain this morning is bigger than any of the three of us." His face chiseled into a stern look.

"I take it there isn't an energy source to be destroyed?" Nolan asked. "What's in the building being guarded?"

Germaine chuckled. "Animals similar to chickens. They have problems with predatory cats that enjoy those chickens, and in the cold season, they always post a guard to look out for the hungry carnivores."

Nolan lowered cross-legged within the branches. "The information you have better be worthwhile," he muttered.

The other two men also lowered themselves into the warmth of the branches until they were closely huddled together. Daniel began to explain in a low voice. "We have told you about the ongoing war between the pureblood races. I am not sure if we have explained the effects. The Celtae race is dying, and as we become better and better at the art of war, we kill more people. In other words, we have become very efficient at the art of death. The enemy is killed as are innocent bystanders in a self-fulfilling war. We fight because it has always been the way we know, and we know no other. In many ways war drives our economies and our culture. It is a difficult thing to change." His voice became louder. "But there is a growing group of people who have a hope for peace. Secretly, we build our momentum across the three remaining races until the day comes when we will rise up and challenge what is now considered a normal way of life."

"I take it both of you are in league with the peace activists?"

"Very much so," Daniel said. "I have seen enough of death, and in the years I have remaining, I give my efforts for peace."

"The Toltec who helped us on Earth, he was also a peace activist, was he not?"

"Yes, and as you have surmised by now, the tattoo is a symbol we carry. It is a ring and within it, a hammer and a sword. The ring is a continuous circle representing the never-ending cycle of life—birth to death to be re-born again. The hammer is a symbol of the builders. It signifies the science which must be part of the peace movement and our knowledge that success relies on more than just hope. The sword over top the hammer reminds us of the strength we need to have to fight for the circle of life and to prosper, fed by the science of man. Centuries ago, the Ionians were the most liberal thinking race when considering peace as an alternative. However, within the Ionians were a smaller group actively pursuing peace, both on a philosophical and scientific level. This is their symbol, long obscured by the blood of so many who lost their lives in the war. Now, we wear it as a silent reminder of what we seek. Our group is called the *Soichaint* and the tattoo is an emblem for others in our growing group to recognize us."

"How do I fit into this Soichaint?" Nolan asked.

"You have strength in you that you do not yet realize. We need you to be part of our movement—if you do in fact believe in life over death as your actions tonight would indicate. The first key is for you to join us. What say you?" Daniel removed his glove and held out his fist.

Germaine followed suit, removing his glove, slapping his hand down while his long fingers surrounded Daniel's clenched fist.

Nolan considered his options. He could go back to Earth and be hunted by the Kaezzar. He could go back to Bailemor and live out a life wondering when would be the next time he would be asked to kill someone just for the sake of killing. Deep inside, he felt cold, not only from the low temperature, but from the chill brought on by fear. Part of him wanted to spring to his feet and run, but another part—the part searching for knowledge and growth, fought off the urge.

The rays of morning sun, slashed between the branches of the trees, sparkling the ice particles hovering in the cold air. A barely audible whistle could be heard as a soft breeze curved through the trees. The wind felt unusually warm to his fingers as Nolan slapped his hand on top of Germaine's. He said in a firm voice, "I'm with you."

Chapter 5

Nolan grimaced as the blue, energy burst slammed into his chest. His green energy shield blocked the burst, dissipating the energy into a shower of colorful sparks. It was the fourth burst he had taken in succession with his shield withstanding the blow each time.

He had performed this test every week since he first attended the Academy, coinciding with the seven weeks since his return from the world of snow and ice. He asked many questions about the Soichaint since their return, but each time Daniel told him to focus on his studies and training. "That is the best he could do for the Soichaint right now," he would say.

Standing at the end of the long narrow room, he saw another burst of energy come from the machine at the opposite end. It took only two seconds for the burst to traverse the 30 yards, and that was barely enough time for him to brace his feet and take a short breath. A grunt was expelled from his lungs as he took two stumbling steps backward, while his energy shield flickered momentarily from the jolt.

A clinical voice came over the speaker system. "That is enough for today, Nolan," the technician said.

The door beside the machine slid open as Nolan willed his energy shield to dissipate. The technician emerged from the other room, scratching his head as he looked up. "That last burst was at 85 per cent of the maximum rating. I've worked here for nine years. In that time, there has only been two others who have been able to take 85 per cent without being knocked against the back wall."

Nolan grinned at the man. "I've been taking some vitamins," he said with a wink.

"Well, whatever it is, keep doing it. Come and see me again the same time next week. Maybe you can set a new record."

Nolan pushed on the door knob, letting himself out into the hallway as he waved a farewell to the technician. He had no intention of setting any records or drawing any unwanted attention to himself. The technician would truly be surprised if he knew the truth. Each day, they took an hour as part of their curriculum to practice the skill of invoking the energy shield. By now, his skills were highly refined, and they were at a much higher level than he let on to the technician. This week, he let the setting go higher before he faked the flicker of his shield. He knew he could take much more than the 85 per cent of maximum he had easily deflected today. If he revealed the extent of his power, the curious would come, and they would investigate. That would not be good for Daniel, and it could be fatal for the Soichaint.

Still having ten minutes to his next class, he took his time walking outdoors across the wide, grass-covered courtyard. He recalled the first day he passed the statues upon his arrival with Germaine. Now, with Deahna's teaching, all the warrior's faces had names.

He spent many long hours with his tutor. In reality, he was a quick study, but asking the extra questions and asking for facts to be explained again, allowed him more time with her. They were good friends, and Nolan sensed she enjoyed his company. The lessons were informal, and he could see in her eyes the happiness when he spoke to her, or when he said something funny, or when he told her how much he cared for her.

The first time he told her of his affection, she blushed, giving her an even higher level of feminine beauty. Nolan remembered his nerves being tense. After all, he had just told his captain he cared for her. The pause had been unnerving. He was relieved when she leaned over and kissed him softly on his cheek.

Nolan brought his hand up to the spot on his cheek, remembering her soft touch. Since then, they continued with his lessons, but they also began to date. Several nights a week they enjoyed each other's company, and on his free days he spent much of that time with her as well. She showed him much of the city and the lifestyle of Bailemor, and at the same time, much about herself.

His thoughts came back to the present as he opened the door of the fighting arena. He stepped through, looking forward to his match with Lukas. Nolan also spent quite a bit of time with the blue-haired man after they had quickly become fast friends. Both of them were in a similar situation, being from different worlds where they left their loved ones behind. Although they would never admit it, considering the strange vanity of men, they both were relieved to have another they could confide in— someone who they could relate to in such a way, allowing them to say they were not alone on this strange world.

As Nolan opened the inner door, the vastness of the arena struck him as it did each time he entered. It was a large circle of flat artificial grass, surrounded by a wooden wall interrupted by gates at several locations. There was seating for some 15 thousand people, but for now, a time for cadet training, those stands were empty.

Sounds of clashing weapons echoed around the round, high, back wall of the arena as various groups of men sparred at different locations. Nolan saw Lukas already waiting for him, staff in hand, near the center of the *Playground* as the floor level of the arena was jokingly nick-named. Seeing Lukas, an instantaneous smile formed on his lips, and his hand waved to the other four cadets who were with his blue-haired friend.

He didn't spend as much time with Jersey or Kelan, who were paired together, or Jennee or Layleen who were the only females of Cadet Squad 33. He liked them all, enjoying their company as part of the squad, and there was a strong bond with each, but it was Lukas he went to, slapping him on the shoulder. "Are you ready?"

"Ready for what?" Lukas replied with a curious frown appearing under his brow of blue hair.

"Ready for me to kick your ass!" Nolan said with a laugh. He held his hand out as Jersey threw him a staff. Hefting it in his hand, he tested its balance. The staff was six feet long and two inches in diameter. Carefully crafted, it was tempered by fire and water in a precarious balance, making the rod strong as iron yet resilient enough to take a solid blow from a like weapon.

Lukas looked over at Instructor Salenson who had just walked up to them from another group. Turning back to Nolan, Lukas mocked, "Unless you've spent some time after class with the sensei, the result will be the same as every other time we have sparred, and that would be with you flat on the ground accepting the offer of my hand to help pick you up off the turf," he reminded his friend.

Sensei had been a word foreign to Lukas and the others from Bailemor. Nolan had used it to describe Salenson, the older, wiry man who still had a quickness and strength about him that easily put fear into his pupils, but he also had a kind heart and the wisdom to know when to show it—and when to show his fighting strength. He took Nolan by the arm, pulling him to the side. "You do remember our conversation earlier today?" the older man asked.

"Yes," Nolan replied. "I've considered your words." He turned back to

Lukas, not telling him his earlier comment was, in fact, accurate. He had indeed been spending extra time with the sensei.

Both Nolan and Lukas put on the thin helmet and the light shin and forearm pads. Realistically, they were effective only in eliminating a killing blow since the leaders of the Academy learned long ago, pain was critical to memory retention. The sting of a blow or the ache of a bruise, was intrinsically corrective.

Both men crouched as the sensei lowered his hand between them, indicating the fight would begin. They circled warily with both holding their staffs across their bodies. Nolan glared at his blue-haired friend. Lukas always began by circling left. He remembered this in addition to most of the other twists, turns and feints Lukas used, but still, he lost each time. The sensei had told him that was, in fact, the problem. *Nolan must anticipate the moves of the combatant, and react to the moves when they happened, but it must happen instinctively. Actions in a fight happen so quickly there isn't time to think—only to do.*

Nolan raised his staff. The vibration rattled his fingers, as Lukas's staff came overtop in a two-handed swing. He had to be quick, turning his body to the right as Lukas's quick reflexes brought the staff around in a short, strong arc toward his right thigh. Nolan pushed his own staff down and to the right, blocking the blow. Nolan stepped back. Both men were once again circling to the left. The first foray had only taken a few seconds.

Lukas smiled.

Nolan saw it. He knew Lukas did it to goad him and to make him lose his concentration. Deep breaths relaxed his mind, but he kept his now well-muscled body on the edge and at the ready.

Nolan stepped forward, planting his right foot as he swung the staff around to Lukas's right leg, but it was a feint. Nolan stopped the movement half-way while now holding his weight on his left foot. He slid his hands down the staff as the wood was pressed toward Lukas's gut in a backhanded thrust. Nolan knew Lukas would come down and block this, and, strategically, he was already spinning on his right toe. However, the recoil from the contact with Lukas's own staff increased the speed of his swing, and Nolan's staff whistled through the air, his body spinning in a tight circle. The staff came in a crashing round house into Lukas's ribs, having been left vulnerable on the left side of his body. Lukas was quick, but his parry only blocked half of the impact from Nolan's staff. The grunt from Lukas's lips told Nolan he surprised the man. Nolan stepped back into his crouch, a satisfied smile forming on his lips.

Lukas grinned through the pain. "That was new—enjoyable. Now that you have my attention, let's get serious."

With that, Lukas came at Nolan with a flurry of lightning-quick moves. He thrust, stabbed and spun in an onslaught of perfect motions. Nolan had seen most of them before, reacting quickly, blocking each blow. When Lukas stepped back into his crouch, Nolan felt only the sting in his left shoulder from a glancing blow. He had done well.

Nolan focused on his breathing and on Lukas's eyes. He had not survived one of Lukas's onslaughts before without having to recover from his knees. Lukas's eyes weren't so jovial now, showing wariness. The blue-haired man came at him again with his onslaught more refined as he showed Nolan heightened respect. Near the end of the flurry, Lukas came at him with two aggressive steps and an overhand swing of the staff.

Nolan was relaxed as he parried the blow. Turning to his left, he knew a forward thrust was coming, and it did. His intuition kicked into high gear as his staff slapped down on Lukas's, slamming it into the ground. Before Lukas could raise his staff, Nolan's right foot slammed down on it. In a combination of blows guided by instinct, Nolan's staff turned into his opponent's gut with a staccato of thuds. Nolan heard the wind knocked from Lukas's lungs that caused him to slouch over. The next overhead blow came from the left side of Nolan's whirling staff onto the blue-haired man's back. Finally, with a lightning-fast reversal, the right end of the staff crashed into the side of Lukas's helmet with a jaw-rattling crunch.

In what appeared to take forever—but was only a few seconds—Lukas's body hung suspended in the air until he finally toppled to the side. Nolan leaned over the man after he had rolled to his back. Lukas's eyes were glazed over. He still panted for breath. His lips mouthed words which did not come. The other members of the squad, and the sensei, also rushed over, making a small circle around the fallen man. Lukas's eyes began to clear as his lips continued to move, but still, only a rasp of air came from his lungs. Nolan and the others bent lower with heightened concern.

A sound finally came from the injured man's lips as he looked from one to the other. "Nolan, you bastard," he said in a voice barely above a hoarse whisper.

On cue, the group burst into laughter as Nolan held down his hand, helping his best friend to his feet.

Lukas twisted his head from side to side, verifying it was still fully attached to his neck. Then he turned to face Nolan. His eyes, for a moment full of disappointment, changed in an instant as a wide smile came across his face. "Well done!" he cried. He took Nolan's hand and held it high in the air. "Never have I seen such speed. I knew you had it in you!" He grinned. His obvious pride in his friend pushed his own pain to the back of his mind.

Nolan knew it was a special moment. He could see Lukas's joy through his own defeat—a sign of a true friend.

Later in the evening, the laughter between the comrades continued. Going into what was their weekend, the six members of Cadet Squad 33 decided to go to a local restaurant for dinner. Afterwards, they moved to the lounge at the back of the establishment for a few drinks, joined there by the late arrival of Daniel and Germaine. Nolan had kept a seat next to him for Deahna who also finally arrived.

It was a good night filled with much laughter and talk of both times of old, and the new times the group shared. Nolan was in his glory with his mentor Daniel close by, and his best friend Lukas sat across from him, while the woman he was infatuated with, held his hand under the table, all night long. Whenever she spoke, he looked at her, fascinated with every part of her being.

As the hours grew longer, first one, then another of the group left the lounge. It was going on midnight when Deahna told Nolan she had to leave. She brought her soft fingers up to cradle his face as she placed a kiss on his cheek. She said, "Ring me tomorrow?" There was a hopeful look in her eye.

"Of course. As soon as I get up."

She backed away, and her arm extended as her fingers slid off his face. She gave him one last bright smile before she turned and scooted out of the room.

Soft music played in the background of the lounge, now empty save for Nolan and Lukas. Lukas had a quizzical look on his face, and he maintained the look for several seconds.

With a nervous laugh Nolan said, "What?"

"You are like a child. Look at you!" he said, leaning back in his chair as his arm waved upward.

"Is it that obvious?"

"Oh, yes." Lukas leaned forward, putting his elbows on the table. "But I envy you. She is wonderful, and your love for her is very noticeable."

Nolan shrugged. "It's something I don't hide. It is what it is."

"How did she react when you told her you loved her?"

"Well, I have told her I *care* for her. I haven't told her I love her, but it *is* obvious," Nolan replied, trying his best not to make it sound apologetic.

Lukas took a drink, feeling the burn of the alcohol as it passed down his throat. "Does she love you?"

Nolan ran his finger around the lip of his glass, looking down into it as he considered the question. "I'm not sure. I hope so, but she's hard to read, at times. There are moments when it's like a wall goes up to avoid the tenderness. I can see it in her eyes."

"Remember, she is also my tutor, so I've seen the look. She is frightened."

A dark thought came across Nolan's mind, and his brow subconsciously furrowed.

Lukas, seeing the look, regained Nolan's confidence before the doubt had even settled. "You didn't see her give *me* a kiss good night, did you?"

Nolan grinned. "You are a good friend. Sure, I have Daniel and Germaine, but their minds are usually off on other things. Deahna—well, what can I say? I do love her, but you are like a brother to me. Our friendship is very important."

Lukas looked down into his drink. "I think our friendship is even more important to me. Those who you mentioned—who are in your life. They are not in mine. I'm here alone except for you, so I'm envious and thankful at the same time."

Not knowing what to say, Nolan stayed silent as he looked up at his friend. He held up a closed fist, thumb up. Lukas chuckled as he made the same fist, pushing it into Nolan's. It was the sign used by the cadets for a job well done.

An odd thought suddenly struck Nolan. Their words and actions sounded vaguely familiar—a memory. Finally, he put his finger on it, remembering the explanation Nolan had given of his bond brother and their relationship.

"Do you know what a bond brother is?" Nolan asked.

"My mentor explained it to me before he left on his mission. There was a bond brother lined up for me, and I met him, but as we talked, all I could think was how ludicrous it was. He was a young man I didn't know, and he knew nothing of me, yet we were to make a sacred commitment to each other. For the rest of our lives we would be there for each other in every way, no matter the circumstances. Before it got too far, I walked out."

Nolan said, "You sound like you know the level of commitment and what it means, and you know me very well."

Lukas raised an eyebrow. "What are you saying?"

"Be my bond brother. I *will* commit to be there for you always, no matter the circumstances."

"You would do that for me?"

"Yes. Even though you have blue hair and a rough manner about yourself which sometimes rubs people the wrong way, I would be honored to be your bond brother." Nolan grinned.

"Then I would commit the same. I will be there when you call on me, no matter the circumstances, even though your hair is the color of the deprived, and you have only bested me once of ten times on the Playground. Yes, I would call you bond brother." This time Lukas held up his fist, thumb up.

Nolan raised his hand, curling his fingers into a fist. He pushed the fist forward until his knuckles cracked into Lukas's. "Indeed, bond brothers until we are taken from this Athar."

Chapter 6

On the salt plains of Kaezzar, a spider called a tambir is the only enemy for the small, red lizards dotting the terrain. The tambir is a unique creature which exemplifies how nature can create the most efficient engineering marvels within the struggle for life itself.

The six-inch long spider has eight legs with four on the front of its body and four on the back. Each leg has a specific, well-defined function. Evolution molded the creature into a burrowing spider, as it would never survive in the escalated daytime temperatures on the surface of the salt plains. Two of its front legs are armed with strong claws. With these, it digs a two-foot-deep burrow, and across the top of the burrow, it spins a grouping of fragile, crisscrossed lines of sticky webbing. On one side of the burrow, it hollows out a small alcove for it to nestle in as it waits.

It doesn't take long for the particles of salt, blown by the wind, to hit and stick to the webbing. Soon after, the burrow is covered with a fragile thin layer of salt, making the hole all but invisible from the surface. Within the alcove, the tambir's two inner, front legs and its two inner, rear legs lift to the roof of the alcove. Small hairs on each of the limbs have very highly-tuned receptors. As the red lizards scurry over top of the plain, these receptors sense the vibrations. The tambir knows when a lizard is moving away or toward the burrow, and it can also sense the speed. Based on the signals sent to its simple brain, the tambir knows exactly when a lizard is about to fall into its lair. As such, it also knows when to coil its outward pair of thick rear legs which will propel it forward to pounce on the lizard before it can scurry back out of the burrow. In this manner, the tambir spider, with its ability to adapt to its surroundings, along with its sense of patience, survives in the inhospitable environment.

The bench shook with a low-frequency vibration as the two atmosphere jets streaked across the skyline of Kaezzar. The jets banked simultaneously to the left, the sudden difference in air pressure across the wings cross section, caused a trail of water vapor to spiral off the far wingtip of each aircraft.

Adrian Korlis sat on the bench across the street from the *Wall of Heroes*, watching the jets veer off until they disappeared from view. Only the vapor trails were left behind.

The city was on high alert. Intelligence reports were predicting another attack on Kaezzar in the next 48 hours, and the report stated a small group of Celtae had hidden themselves in the northern mountain range. This mountain range was really a line of sharp pinnacles of rock forced upward, centuries before, when the planet had split as it cooled during its formation process. There were numerous places to hide in the 200-mile-long range. Supposedly, the Celtae had built a portable power generator and were charging and stocking an armory of laser weapons within their lair. The aircraft, just crossing the yellow sky, carried heat-seeking sensors, and were on their way to the range to try and locate the enemy hideout.

The bench vibrated again, but this time because of a person sitting down on the other end of it. Adrian Korlis's gaze lowered from the sky to the Wall of Heroes. Without turning to Julian, who now sat beside him, he said, "How many names do you think are on the wall?"

Julian shrugged. "I've been told there are over five hundred thousand names, but then the wall was only constructed 80 years ago. There are many more Kaezzar soldiers who have died in the war since its beginning."

Adrian picked this spot for their meeting because he didn't want to be overheard. The sidewalk in front of them was busy with many people walking back and forth on their lunch hour. He knew, with the background hustle and bustle of this less than private spot, they were less likely to be conspicuous and overheard than if they were in a more secluded location.

Adrian stretched his false lower leg. It had been some time since the blast removed the bottom of his limb, but the knee still stiffened up if he didn't move it from time to time. "Six more names will be added," he said. "There were six body bags returned from Earth. You remember—the mission you told me not to worry about. The one you told me you would update me on if anything critical occurred." Adrian turned, offering a cold stare to Julian.

Julian took a couple of deep breaths. "Things got out of control. Unfortunately, casualties do happen, from time to time, in our line of business. I didn't want to bother you with details. I'm sure you have more important things to take care of." He lifted his eyes, forcing a smile, albeit a cold one.

Adrian did not blink. His words came quietly. "Save the smile for some other moron. You are done. I'm going to break you down so far you will be fortunate if you're not in jail before the end of the week."

An instinctive puckering of Julian's sphincter along with the tone of his superior's voice, caused him to draw back. His smile faded as he turned white. He shifted and leaned against the back of the bench while focusing on the far wall filled with the names of the dead. He took another deep breath as the color returned to his face, and in a shaky voice, said, "Now that you mention jail, I visited the Bolivar Steam Plant three days ago. I met some interesting people there—"

Adrian's gaze turned ice cold.

"—including your brother."

"My brother died years ago in the war…"

"No!" Julian interrupted. He turned to match Adrian's cold stare with an added touch of cruelty. "You would like people to think your brother died, but he didn't. He is incarcerated at Bolivar. I saw him with my own eyes. Do you think I'm a fool?"

Adrian looked furtively at the people on the sidewalk. "Keep your voice lower," he said through gritted teeth.

Julian smiled triumphantly. He knew he had the man. "I *bet* you want me to keep my voice down. It wouldn't be good for the Senate to know their chief officer of the Watch, a former hero of the war, has a brother in jail."

"We need to have an understanding, then. I will ignore the dead from Earth, and you will ignore my brother's present accommodations," Adrian proposed.

Julian smiled. He had his superior on the run. "I want more. If you love your brother—resign. Recommend me as your successor. You've been in my way for far too long." He swallowed to control his drool as he went in for the killing blow.

Adrian shifted nervously. "That will not work. Think about it. There are two in front of you within the sector commanders who are rated as more promotable. If I suddenly resigned, and you were recommended, the others who were overlooked would surely investigate. They would quickly discover both the body bags from Earth and my brother's incarceration."

Julian's lips shifted against his teeth as he tried to find a flaw in the man's words, but he knew the general was right. He finally spit out the words. "Then you had better come up with another way to get me out of your hair."

"There is something."

Julian looked to Adrian, raising an eyebrow.

"As you know, the efforts at subverting the war effort are growing. It has not gone un-noticed by the Senator for War. He is pulling together a special task force to deal with and quell the subversion. He has asked me for a recommendation for the head of the task force, who would hold the rank of general."

General! Julian thought, having difficulty not blurting it out. *What an opportunity! That would make me an equal rank with Korlis—the hero of the people.* "I like your way of thinking," he said.

"I can see why you would, but this promotion will come at a high price. If I make the personal recommendation, your actions are a reflection on me. I put myself at risk, and it's a risk that will not happen for free."

"What would you want from me so that you proceed with the recommendation?" Julian asked warily.

"The senator responsible for the war effort also carries the portfolio for the penal system. If you receive the appointment, you will be in his inner circle, and you will have influence—influence enough to get my brother released."

Julian crossed his leg over his knee. His fingers tapped against the back of the bench. He didn't want to give the impression he was anxious even though his brain screamed for him to yell his agreement. After a few moments he responded, "I agree."

Adrian quickly replied, "You should hear something within a few days, so good luck." He held his hand out to his subordinate.

With disdain, Julian pushed his hand out and shook Adrian's. His overwhelming feeling of success told him to just get up and leave the man sitting with that dumbfounded look on his face, but he wanted to play this out further. As he shook his hand, Julian knew he would have Jelan Tulis released, but to him. Tulis would be right beside him on the task force. He was a big man, and there would be assignments requiring his type of brute strength. Of even more importance, he wanted to keep a very close eye on him. He smiled at Adrian as he slid off the bench and walked back toward the Watch building. His head was held high as he was quite happy with himself and his impending progress up the political ladder.

Adrian watched Julian walk away until he was lost in the bustle of the crowded sidewalk. He smiled, trying to hold back the chuckle. *It took a while for you to finally take the bait,* he thought, *but now you are securely on the line.* He remembered back to the past few weeks. It was not hard to discover the phone taps at his home by Luis Ortez. He knew it was only a matter of time before they hacked into his computer. The Jelan Tulis file was hidden on his computer behind some simple passwords. He knew it would not take long for the information to get to Julian.

Jelan Tulis was not his brother. He closed his eyes for a moment at the memory. His brother had indeed died in the war. His own leg was also gone, and for what—the honor of having your name scribed on the Wall of Death? His moist eyes opened as he again looked at the numerous names spattered on what was really referred to as the Wall of Heroes.

In his younger days, he had little patience, but lying in the hospital for three months while waiting for the pain to leave his leg—waiting for the false feelings and sensations to stop, had given him time to understand patience. Now, as the senior member of the Soichaint on Kaezzar, he needed to instill the same patience into all his operatives, including Jelan Tulis.

Jelan Tulis had surgery 12 months ago. A minor adjustment of the nose and a sharpening of the chin had surprising results. The newly-created resemblance to Adrian's own face was uncanny. Jelan had volunteered for the assignment, knowing he could be in prison for quite some time before the events would play out. He had been there six months when Julian had finally come to visit.

Adrian rose to a standing position as his one well-muscled leg sprung him up. He walked toward the Watch building, remembering the satisfied and unwitting step of Julian. Adrian knew the young man was a fool—just the fool the Soichaint wanted to head the task force. The man was so easy to read. If all went as planned, Jelan would be kept very close to him. Adrian knew that condition was the only way Julian would get permission to pardon Jelan. *It was a good day,* he thought. The wind blew across Adrian Korlis's body while the hairs on his arms and on the back of his neck pushed up on end. He thought to himself, *yes, my overconfident young friend—you have moved much too quickly, and now, much like the unwitting red lizards of the salt plains, you have fallen into my lair.*

Chapter 7

Nolan stepped up the short ladder toward the cockpit of the small, sleek jet. Once at the top rung, he slipped one leg over the fuselage followed by the other. With a hand braced on each side bulkhead, he lowered himself into the cramped space he would occupy for the next hour and a half. As the pilot's assistant secured the harnesses over his chest, he looked out and saw both Daniel and Germaine on the smooth tarmac bathed by the early morning sunrise.

Nolan's palms were sweaty within his thin flight gloves. This was the premier event bringing a close to the *Graduation Games*. The circuit flight pitted the best Akkadian flyer against the best the Gwyneddmen had to offer. In earlier fly-offs, he bested his fellow cadets for the honor of flying for the Akkadians against the much-heralded Dragon Treve.

Dragon was just now walking from the hanger toward his jet parked beside the craft Nolan was sweating in. The Gwyneddman had short-cropped, black hair and deep-set, dark eyes. His features were sharp, giving him a hawk-like appearance, apropos for this event that would soar them not only to new heights in the air but also within the hearts of the thousands who would be cheering them on from the finish line.

Dragon's father, General Treve, walked with him with his hand on his son's shoulder as he gave last minute advice. The older man was thinner than his son but carried similar facial features. The crown of General Treve's head was devoid of growth and ringed by a short, neatly trimmed band of white hair. Notwithstanding this, there was no mistaking Dragon was surely his father's son.

The general's first name was long forgotten as his exploits of bravery in the war had moved him up the military hierarchy. He was now the highest ranking Gwyneddman in the military of Bailemor. Consequently, when people mentioned "The General" there was no confusion about who they were referring to. As he came closer to the jet, Nolan could see Dragon's irritated features as he faced away from his father, while the older man dramatically waved his hand back and forth in last minute instruction to his son. Dragon scooted up the ladder and lowered himself into the cockpit of his jet. His dark, ice-cold stare toward Nolan was sinister. The young Gwyneddman had a lot of pressure on him and took the Games very seriously.

Held annually, the Graduation Games were one of the biggest sporting events on the world of Crann Bith. Graduates from both the Akkadian and Gwynedd academies were pitted against each other in a series of events to show the people of Bailemor the prowess of the top students. Events exhibiting their prowess in combat, accuracy and speed were the preamble to this—the main event known as the flying circuit.

As the glass cockpits closed on the two jets, Nolan thought back to the first time he met Dragon two days earlier. Lukas had just won the gold pin in the staff event, and Nolan was due to fight Dragon in the finals of hand-to-hand combat. Their fight consisted of three, two-minute rounds. They both fought very well, giving and taking solid blows that stung despite the protective gear and padded gloves they wore. At the end of the fight, Nolan had a bloodied nose while Dragon brandished a cut over his left eye. The crowd in the arena cheered their efforts, and the cheer redoubled to an exuberant roar as the spectators agreed with the judges who called the fight a draw.

However, it was an understatement to say Dragon wasn't happy with this result. The referee pulled up both their hands, signifying the decision, but Dragon dragged his hand clear and turned to face Nolan. It was the first time Nolan had seen the ice-cold stare just before the young, hot-headed Gwyneddman stormed off the Playground.

A low-pitched beep brought Nolan's mind back to the jet. A voice came over the two-way radio integrated into his colorful, light-blue helmet.

"This is Jason Rider. I am the referee for this event. If you look up at your 11:00, you will see I'm already airborne."

Nolan pulled down the silver-plated goggles and looked up, seeing the referee's high-power flyer making a slow turn over the airfield.

The static-coated voice came over the radio again. "The course is 420 miles long, and there are nine markers in the circuit. You must target every marker before moving to the next one. All of the markers are loaded into your radar. The race is timed, and there are penalties. If I see questionable maneuvers, I will deduct time intervals up to ten seconds—my call. If you miss a marker, you will be deducted seconds based on the distance. The standard is one second for every five feet off the mark. Is that understood?"

Dragon responded first. "Gold Bird understands."

Nolan was next. "All clear to Blue Bird," he said.

Both of the jets were painted ceremonially with the colors of their clan. Nolan's jet had a metallic coat of royal-blue paint covering the 25-foot-long fuselage. The span of the 30-degree, raked-back wings was also 25 feet. In aerodynamics classes, at the Academy, he had learned symmetry was important for high-speed flight. At the end of the airfoil section of the wing were numerous reverse scallops, giving the illusion of teeth along the trailing edge. There was a thin band of light blue paint at this edge, highlighting the serrations. A similar pattern and color were on the vertical tail and the fin bisecting its ten-foot height.

Dragon's jet was a copy of Nolan's except the color was gold. The paint had triangular pigments in it, giving the gold a wide variety of shades, depending on the angle of the light refracting within the thin layer. Nolan was envious of Dragon's jet. He thought to himself, *I hope your jet doesn't fly as good as it looks.*

Both twin-turbine engines that took up most of the space within the fuselage, roared into life simultaneously, pushing a momentary orange flame out the rear exhaust. With Dragon taking the lead, Nolan released the brake and taxied out behind the Gwynedd jet as the sun's rays played on the gold flakes of paint seeming to bring the jet to life. Each jet turned onto the wide runway and parked on the painted spot assigned to it. This was the starting point for the race where Dragon took one last look at Nolan before arrogantly flicking down his visor.

"Five seconds," the referee said over the radio.

With his left foot on the brake and his left hand holding the directional stick jutting up out of the floor of the cockpit, his right hand slowly increased the throttle. The jet angled nose down as the brakes struggled to hold the jet in position.

"Start!" The referee's loud voice boomed over the radio.

Nolan lifted his foot off the brake, and the jet catapulted forward. He increased the throttle smoothly to 75 per cent. Two hundred yards down the runway, he pulled back lightly on the stick and maintained a level flight 20 feet off the ground. The throttle was then increased to 85 per cent, and when his speed hit 220 miles an hour, he pulled back hard on the stick. The jet shot up and off to the right toward the first marker 60 miles away.

Swiveling his head in a circle, Nolan spotted Dragon just behind him and to the left. *It was an excellent start,* Nolan thought. He kept his throttle set to 85 per cent, not wanting to give everything away this early in the race. No doubt Dragon was doing the same in the cat and mouse event.

Nolan removed his focus from Dragon. He knew the result of this event would be based on what *he* did, not what his opponent endeavored to do. He adjusted the trim tabs of the rear stabilizer, removing some of the pressure off his arm holding the stick. The assent was smooth with only the occasional buffeting from turbulent air. He paid close attention to the turbulence, noting in his mind the altitudes that were clean. The air speed was also important. He watched it closely as he leveled out the aircraft at 20 thousand feet and took additional care to ensure his air speed stabilized at 320 miles an hour.

Out of the corner of his eye, Nolan saw Dragon go higher. This event was quite unique, proving the skill of flying was not just elaborate maneuvers. Finding the right conditions at different altitudes was critical to winning when one considered the two aircraft were identical in performance. The skill of the flyer was in finding the tailwinds, reducing the turbulence and making every motion of the jet smooth and uneventful.

Both planes smoothly flew from altitude to altitude until each pilot was satisfied with his craft's position. Nolan had settled for 28 thousand feet while Dragon was cruising three thousand feet below him. Dragon was slowly pulling away, but this didn't disturb Nolan who knew it was much too early in the race to panic. In his estimation, the difference was only two seconds, and the first marker was still a few minutes away.

Looking out at the horizon, all Nolan could see was the red haze, broken here and there by clumps of giant trees, stretching through the haze for the sunlight. The sky was clear with a front of clouds off to the east, but it wouldn't be close enough to bother them today.

A dull beep sounded in Nolan's cockpit. Looking at the radar screen, the first marker had begun to flash, and the second marker became visible. At the bottom of the screen the marker's altitude was shown – *24 thousand feet.*

"Freaking hell," Nolan whispered to himself. By chance, Dragon was at the right altitude. Nolan would need to drop slowly, meaning he would lose more time, but here again, he didn't panic. He veered slowly to the right and began his descent, keeping out of Dragon's turbulent wake.

The markers were fascinating pieces of technology. They were a five-foot-diameter sphere with four internal engines receiving global data regarding the marker's position. The marker was able to hover in the same position while compensating for wind speed. It gave out an invisible, electromagnetic field for an accurate radius of 30 yards from the marker's central core. If the jet flew through the electromagnetic field, a signal would be sent to the jet identifying a hit. The tricky part was to make a hit without hitting the sphere.

Nolan was above and to the right of Dragon. Dragon flew through the electromagnetic field just to the right of the marker, then veered north toward the next target. Nolan followed to the left of the marker as a high-pitched beep signaled he had also hit the electromagnetic zone.

Rider's voice came over the radio. "Both jets had clean hits. No time penalties. Dragon is six seconds in the lead."

Nolan frowned as he concentrated on his flying. The next four legs were uneventful, but he was slowly making up time. As they hit marker six at an altitude of five thousand feet, he was only two seconds behind. Directionally, they were now flying back toward Bailemor. Nolan was flying at 30 thousand feet, and because of the thinner air, his airspeed was faster. However, he knew he would lose some time when he made a quick descent to the next marker at eight thousand feet.

Suddenly, there was a splash of gold filling the window of the cockpit as Dragon's jet crossed Nolan's path not 20 yards in front of him, pummeling his jet with a violent rush of turbulent air. Pulling the stick back and to the right, Nolan's jet went into a wide barrel roll. Two thousand feet lower, when Nolan had righted the craft, he saw the gold jet screaming in a controlled descent to the marker. He could immediately tell Dragon had increased his throttle close to 100 per cent. The Gwyneddman was making his move.

There was a crackle on the radio as Dragon's voice was heard. "My apologies—bad thermal."

Nolan punched the throttle forward as he screamed into the microphone attached to the helmet, "Appeal! Appeal!"

Nolan looked up to his right, seeing the referee's jet. The words crackled over the earpiece, "Denied. Dragon is eight seconds ahead."

Nolan slammed his fist into the side window. *Freaking hell*, he thought. *It seems there is a handicap when competing against a general's son.* He refocused on his jet, checking the controls, ensuring they were optimized as he followed Dragon down to the marker. He knew he still had four more legs to catch up to the young Gwyneddman.

Nolan flew flawlessly for the next and longest leg of the circuit. He kept to the higher altitudes, and it gave him an advantage. The controls were not as responsive at those heights, but his superior flying skills kept the movements of the craft smooth. Once again, he was only two seconds behind Dragon as they both hit the next marker without penalties. In the eyes of the referee, both had flown a clean flight thus far.

The next section was the toughest on the course. Both aircraft would need to make a steep dive toward the next marker that was only 200 feet above the level of the plateau. The marker was hovering at the entrance to a main boulevard of a once thriving city, now long dead. Neither one of the flyers could see the marker, as it was within the red haze covering the first 300 feet above the plateau. This portion of the flight, from this marker to the next at the far end of the boulevard, was to be flown blind with only instrumentation and radar to guide them.

Just in front of him, Nolan saw Dragon pull up his aircraft's nose just before he disappeared into the haze. He was close behind when he buffeted into the layer of red dust particles, but he didn't notice, as he was already focused completely on his instruments. The screen on the right side of the panel showed the flashing marker just in front of him. It also indicated Dragon about to pass through its electromagnetic field while also revealing the location of the next marker seven miles ahead. The second radar screen on the left that he had turned on just prior to entering the red haze, gave a hazy image of the once majestic but now crumbled buildings dotting both sides of the long thoroughfare.

Nolan was concentrating on the radar when wet spatter rattled into the front of his jet. He ducked instinctively just as both radar screens flickered, then went dead. He knew right away what Dragon had done. The Gwyneddman had dumped his emergency fuel tank, and the liquid had flooded his radar sensors. Nolan's fingers tightened around the control stick, not daring to move it. He knew the safest course was to hold the stick steady, hoping he would hear the high-pitched beep of the next marker. Then he would pitch the aircraft up vertically.

After five nervous seconds, the radar screens flickered back into life, showing a building right in front of him. He hit the control stick hard to the right as the plane turned onto its side and just cleared the side of the structure. Another ominous form showed directly in front of the jet. This time Nolan crashed the stick hard to the left. He heard a metallic *clink* as something scraped the underside of the fuselage. He fought for control with the jet in a wild turn, slicing through the red haze and back onto the edge of the boulevard. But his speed was too great, and his angle was unfavorable.

He only had one chance to hit the marker. Pulling the stick back to the right, his left hand released the air brakes, forcing the jet into a skid through the air in a sidelong tail slide.

Nolan waited for the high-pitched beep, but it didn't come. "Shit!" he yelled over the radio.

He pulled back the stick and punched the throttle forward as he retracted the air brakes.

The referee's voice came over the radio. "Nolan Harrison has a three second penalty for missing the mark."

Nolan slapped the glass side window again. The three second penalty didn't bother him as much as the sight of Dragon's gold jet. Shooting out of the red haze, he could see Dragon was easily eight seconds ahead. There were eleven seconds of valuable time to make up with only two legs of the circuit remaining. He had a notion of what he had to do, and it formulated through his logical mind into a plan. It was risky, but it was the only chance he had to win. He pulled the stick back, heading for the heavens.

Dragon was smug in his jet, cutting through the air at an altitude of eight thousand feet—the same altitude as the last marker that was already flashing on his radar. At the marker he would need to put his jet into a tight turn. Nothing complicated was required. At first, he thought Nolan had conceded as the Akkadian accelerated to a higher altitude. Nolan was only three seconds behind, but he was cruising at 35 thousand feet. Dragon laughed as he shook his head. The Akkadian had obviously lost his mind or his radar. Being at that high an altitude would make it impossible to hit this upcoming marker.

When it rains, it pours, Nolan thought. The metallic *clink* he had heard was not uneventful. Behind him, he saw a thin line of heated gas coming from his left engine. He quickly concluded a sharp object must have loosened the turbine cover, and the hot gas, critical for his thrust, was spilling inefficiently into the air. It gave him another reason to go for higher altitude. With the lower temperature at the greater height, the seal on the panel that had been jarred, fit tighter. When he had passed through eight thousand feet on his climb, the most he could get from the engines was 75 per cent thrust. Here, cruising at 35 thousand feet, the thrust needle was tickling 100 per cent. His only problem was how to hit the marker so far below him.

Dragon was already thinking about his victory celebration. *Yes!* he thought. After the turn at the marker, there was a short cruise to the bridge spanning the chasm between the Summit and the Akkadian Upper City.

This was the finish line, and he was so far ahead, he planned to do a barrel roll over top the bridge to the cheers of the thousands of spectators who would be watching from the walls on either side. The people of Bailemor, especially those carrying binoculars, would be given an exhibition of his flying prowess.

With a slight movement of the stick, he veered to the right, then pitched the jet on its side. This was followed by a slow pull back on the directional stick. He was going to execute a tail slide around the marker before shooting for home.

Halfway through the turn, the smile on Dragon's face turned to a look of curiosity, as he heard a high-pitched whine. Looking at the controls, he couldn't see anything wrong, but the whine was growing in intensity. Then, Dragon's eyes grew wide, almost popping out of his head. He barely saw the blur of Nolan's blue plane as it came down at a 45-degree angle, screaming past only feet above his cockpit. Red lights all over the instrument panel came on as the wake of Nolan's plane buffeted Dragon's jet. Dragon fought for control as his left engine stalled.

Nolan was pressed back into his seat while his face rippled with contortions from the gravitational force of the dive. He tried to keep from blacking out as he saw the air speed indicator click over 400 miles an hour. He heard the quick beep of the marker as miraculously, he caught it. He pulled up on the stick, knowing this would be close. The plane thundered toward the haze and the hard plateau just under it. He kept constant pressure on the controls, and little by little, the jet responded. The bottom of its arc trailed black smoke from the damaged turbine, but the jet survived as it just kissed the top of the red haze before rebounding upward.

Dragon scrambled in his jet as his face also contorted, but in this instance, it was because of the rage he felt. He re-fired the stalled engine and pushed the jet back to full throttle while following Nolan's damaged jet.

If Nolan was going to win, it would only be because of his jet's momentum from the almost suicidal dive he just completed. The one damaged engine had not survived and was now billowing out a thick stream of black smoke. His thrust was only 50 per cent, and as a result, his airspeed was reducing, but the bridge was now in sight. He held a steady hand on the controls as he willed the plane to the finish line, knowing he had to finish ahead by at least three seconds because of his earlier penalty.

The crowd of 40 thousand people watched the race with thunderous cheers and whoops from Akkadian and Gwyneddman alike. The blue streak, angling downward to the bridge, was Nolan Harrison. The gold flash, which was catching up quickly, was Dragon Treve. The blue streak crossed over the bridge followed very quickly by the gold flash.

On the ground, the Event Announcer's voice came over the speaker system. "Blue crossed ahead of gold by 4.3 seconds. Blue wins by 1.3 seconds!"

Nolan heard the announcement and whooped in triumph, ironically, just as the gold Gwynedd aircraft thundered past him. Nolan pulled back the throttle to 30 per cent. He patted the instrument panel with a loving hand, whispering, "You did great girl. You're some machine."

Nolan coddled the jet back to the airfield, bringing it to a gentle stop in front of the hanger, where he saw Dragon's gold jet abandoned at the end of the runway. The canopy had been flung off and was upside down on the paved surface. It appeared the young man had left his craft hastily, not even bothering to bring it back to the hanger. There was no sign of him or any of his supporters. Nolan shrugged as he turned off the one good engine. He climbed out of the cockpit, jumping down to the tarmac where he saw both Daniel and Germaine walking out toward him.

"Congratulations!" Daniel hollered with a wide smile.

Coming within range, Germaine slapped Nolan on the shoulder. "We saw the race on the viewer. I don't think I would have kept my focus as well as you did, considering the less than honorable maneuvers Dragon pulled." He shook his head.

"Where is Dragon? I have a few words for him," Nolan said, lowering an eyebrow.

Daniel smiled smugly. "He slammed his helmet back into the cockpit of his jet and left in a big hurry. Seeing the result of the race, his father left before he touched down. That seemed to frustrate Dragon even more. He was last seen storming out in that direction." His finger pointed toward the double doors at the far end of the hanger.

"Best you leave him alone," Germaine added. "Facing his father will be enough punishment for how he behaved in the air."

Nolan turned to the hanger and saw five people walking briskly out toward them. "Who are they?"

"News people and video people. You are now quite famous. That was the best race in quite some time," Daniel stated.

Nolan made it through the multitude of questions from the interviewers.

Suddenly, Earth was on all their lips—the home world of the Blue Flyer! He took it in stride, embarrassed by the attention, but at the same time, he was proud others looked up to him. He was truly part of the Akkadian clan.

It didn't take long for Daniel to cut the questions short, stating Nolan had to get ready for the Graduation Games Banquet later in the evening. He whisked Nolan away to the chagrin of the interviewers who were fascinated with the story they hoped to create from the Earthman's mysterious past.

Once at Daniel's house, Nolan was quick to call Deahna on the computer's communication mode. He dialed in her number and when her face popped into the screen, he couldn't hold back his smile. "Looks like our table might be busy tonight," he proudly said.

She smiled and pulled her fingertips to her lips, applying a light kiss. Turning her hand, she brought her fingertips to the screen. "Congratulations. You did very well, but you had me worried. Some of your maneuvers were very dangerous." A crease came across her brow.

"No fears now," Nolan offered, making his smile even wider in an effort to dispel her concerns.

Deahna shook her head. "I do worry about you. You've finished the Academy. Now what? You don't seem like the kind of man who will open a shoe store." There was a hint of irritation in Deahna's voice.

Nolan's eyebrows stooped. "I thought you would be happy for me."

"I'm very happy that you did so well—celebrity status," Deahna said with a touch of sarcasm. "Every wing of the military service will be trying to recruit you now."

"Is that a bad thing?"

Deahna replied, "No, not really. After all, the war has gone on for so long, what's another death?"

Nolan was at a loss for words. "You care about me?"

Deahna's eyes became soft as she brought her fingers to the screen once more, dragging them down the side. "I'll see you at the banquet tonight," she said softly. Then the screen went blank, replaced by the words - *Connection terminated.*

Nolan pushed back the chair. His feelings were mixed. He was happy with the result of the race, as were the majority of the Akkadians, but perhaps Deahna was right. He needed to be wary not to be pushed into something he didn't want to be part of. The race had been dangerous, but no one else's life was in the balance. He wasn't dropping a bomb, nor was he shooting at anyone. He just came to the realization, as Deahna had done some time ago, that in all likelihood the Akkadians would try and utilize his skills for the war. The thought worried Nolan as did the wall he saw put up by Deahna. It wasn't getting lower. Rather, it was growing. He knew, soon, he would have to bring the topic of his love for the woman directly into her face. She needed to understand exactly how he felt.

The banquet began at 6:00 in the evening. There was an excellent meal, presentations and many boring speeches. Nolan was sitting with Daniel, Germaine, Lukas and Deahna as well as the other members of Cadet Squad 33. He was happy when he went up to receive his gold pin for winning the flying competition—almost as happy as he was for Lukas when he went up to receive his pin for the staff fighting event. As much as he was satisfied with his own achievements, he was ecstatic with the results of the team. Both he and Lukas had won gold while Jersey had won a silver pin in his competition. Three awards from one squad were unheard of.

Consequently, even though the Gwynedd had won their share of pins, there were more than a few long faces at the Gwynedd tables. Dragon was conspicuous by his absence, and his father, the general, was not amused, knowing everyone was thinking the question, but none were daring enough to ask where his son was.

Nolan also became quickly frustrated. He had hoped to spend some time alone with Deahna. He needed to tell her how he felt, and he needed to hear her response, but there was never a quiet moment at their table. One after the other, Akkadian supporters came over to congratulate him. Others sat and already, as Deahna had forecasted, began to recruit him to different vocations. Here and there he was able to steal a look at her. She would smile, and it would give him the strength to handle the barrage of people, and she seemed to know he needed her support. Whenever he thought his frustration level was about to burst, he would feel her hand on his shoulder. It calmed him, but by the end of the night, Nolan had enough. He had been polite for long enough. If he forced a smile for one more person, he thought surely his face would be forever cast in the silly-looking grin.

Finally, he rose to his feet and looked to Daniel. "I need some air. I'll wait outside until you and Deahna are ready." Without waiting for a reply, he turned from the table, brushing his fingers across Deahna's shoulder as he moved toward the exit.

Nolan took quick steps to the side door, knowing it would be quiet there.

Others still yelled their congratulations as he pushed the door open, then stepping into the darkness of the night. As he pressed the door closed behind him, the metallic *click* of the latch brought much needed silence—something he hadn't heard in several hours. He leaned back against the door with his hand still on the long round handle, exhaling in relief.

After a few moments, he spied a short wall on the other side of the laneway and moved over to it. He would sit and wait for his friends, but the silence was broken by the chirp of birds from a group of trees at the side of the laneway. Nolan became alert, knowing the birds had been disturbed. It didn't take long for the three figures to move from the shadow of the branches while their faces were lit up by the starlight overhead.

"Hello, Dragon," Nolan said warily as he rose to his feet.

Dragon paced slowly back and forth in front of his two friends. "You certainly are polite, Blueblood, and much more courteous than you were up in the air when you almost ripped the top of my jet off!" His eyes flared with anger.

"You seem to forget about your mysterious thermal and the fuel load you dropped on me," Nolan replied.

"Do you know who I am, Blue? It was bad enough we succumbed to a draw in our hand-to-hand fight, but do you know what it's like for the general's son to lose? You have no idea." Dragon answered his own question while shaking his head from side to side.

"It's over, Dragon, so forget about it."

Dragon walked closer to Nolan, followed by his two henchmen. "It's not over until I beat you, and that will be right now." He pulled back his coat, flipping the tail over his hip. There was a long knife in a sheath at his belt. The Gwyneddman snapped his fingers at one of his cohorts who also pulled back his jacket. The sequence of events must have been planned out in advance as Dragon's companion pulled the long knife from his sheath and threw it to Nolan's feet.

Nolan moved to a squat, picking up the knife. His exhale broke the still night as he slowly rose back up to his full height. "Three against one. Is this how a general's son usually fights his battles?" If he did have to fight, he wanted his opponent distracted. Dragon's temper would help him.

Dragon's eyes went wide, and his knuckles turned white as his grip strangled the handle of the knife. He shuffled closer to Nolan, knees bent and at the ready. Noise and light burst from the door as it was flung open.

Daniel and Deahna, waving their good-byes, backed out of the doorway. The door closed, and as they both turned, they were surprised by the scene before them. Daniel walked toward Nolan in a wide semi-circle, keeping Deahna at his back. He said in a deep, no-nonsense tone, "What's going on, Nolan?"

"This is none of your business, old man!" Dragon cut in.

"I am making it my business," Daniel firmly replied. "You have been beaten. That is bad enough, but to have an illegal duel during the festivities, and a duel pitting three on one, should be beneath you. That would not go over well with the Akkadians. Not even your own Gwyneddmen would be able to ignore the stink of cowardice it brings." While he talked, Daniel opened his jacket pushing it around his hip.

Dragon saw the small laser pistol in the holster at Daniel's belt. He also heard both his friends take a step back. Showing his frustration, his eyes rattled in their sockets, and his arm flung forward, shaking. The tip of the long knife pointed at Nolan. "This isn't the end of our issue, Blueblood!" he screamed. "The old man won't always be here to protect you!" Dragon turned before stomping off into the darkness with his two henchmen close behind.

After a few seconds, making sure they were gone, Daniel slipped the knife from Nolan's fingers and flung it into the bushes. Deahna leaned against Nolan, and her eyes searched up to his. For a brief second Nolan thought he saw the feelings deep inside her. He saw the love, but he also saw her fear. Just as quickly as it was there, it was gone. Deahna recovered, forcing a smile, once again protected within the walls surrounding her heart. She took Nolan's hand, and the three of them walked out of the laneway toward home.

Long after they left, the birds gave out several curt chirps. A cloaked figure shifted in the darkness. A glow formed as he inhaled on the pipe, lighting up his long, thin, hooded face. *Very interesting,* he thought. Peron had also seen the look in the woman's eyes, and he realized it was the weakness he had been looking for.

Chapter 8

It was now three months since Nolan had arrived at Bailemor on the world of Crann Bith. He graduated with honors from the Skills Academy with a special commendation for his flying prowess, and now, one week after the graduation ceremonies, there were numerous suitors knocking on his door with requests for his services. High-ranking recruiters came from almost every wing of the military, and they told him he would be invaluable toward their effort in the war. Nolan would listen politely, telling them he would respond with his decision as soon as there was one.

There were also private entrepreneurs who wooed him with vast amounts of money and high levels of responsibility. In his efforts to keep clear of the war, Nolan investigated these offers closely. He found the same discovery every time, and that discovery led him to a generalized conclusion. With the war effort being so far-reaching and so entrenched in the culture of these people, every business was in some way associated with the war. Each time he investigated one of these companies, he would find they were supplying material to the military, or they were financed by the military. The never-ending trail back to the war left Nolan disillusioned and unemployed.

However, he was popular, and that popularity grew. Within his squad, even though most of them had taken positions within the fighting elite, they looked to him as their leader. His confidence continued to grow, and although he couldn't really understand why, he thrived on the allegiance of the others. Even though he saw the squad members take excellent positions, he wasn't yet ready to take that leap. Only Lukas and he remained as holdouts.

From time to time he would move in the higher circles of the Bailemor elite. The more often than not obnoxious bureaucrats who populated the political wing of the military never tired of hearing the story of the blueblood from Earth who not only bested but outwitted the cream of the Gwynedd cadets. Usually, Nolan would have Lukas tag along with him since the bureaucrats tended to steer clear of his friend and his frock of shocking, blue hair, but Lukas, neither shy nor particular, would barge into anyone's conversation. He often told Nolan that was the price they had to pay for his story and the subtle changes he made each time he told it. The two men even developed a language of sarcastic facial expressions. At these upper-crust gatherings they couldn't blurt out their real feelings, but even across a room, with a droop of an eyebrow, or a twist of a lip, they were able to decipher each other's impressions of the company they kept.

The purposeless activities occupied Nolan's time with the hope that one day he would be called upon by the Soichaint to support the peace movement. He pestered Daniel endlessly, but the older man told him his time would come. He was to keep his skills honed so that, when he was called upon, he could be effective. Daniel told him many times that he was a key to their peace plan.

However, on this day, Nolan put thoughts of Daniel, Lukas and the war behind him, having made a special date with Deahna. His hand rested on her far hip as they walked from the bullet station along one of the many dirt roads crisscrossing the western half of the Akkadian Lower City. Here, in the bright sunshine, the agricultural district flourished. Vegetables and fruits were grown while the Bailemorian version of poultry and beef were fattened to provide meat to the population.

They walked on the dirt road for ten minutes as it narrowed into nothing more than a laneway. The green and yellow shards of grass became longer as less human trampling made it this far into the heart of the fruit district.

Deahna's steps mimicked Nolan's, and their bodies moved cohesively as they sauntered along the laneway. Without turning her head, she said, "When are you going to tell me where we're going?"

"When we get there. It's a surprise," he replied cheerfully.

Deahna was in an exceptionally good mood. She turned her face to Nolan, pressing her lips to his cheek in a kiss. "Okay," she said through her wide, carefree smile. The feelings inside her comprised that rare moment where she wanted to go forward and not move at the same time. She knew the surprise ahead would be wonderful, yet as the slight breeze blew her red hair back, allowing the early morning sun to warm her forehead, she didn't want the peace of the moment to end.

They walked for five more minutes before Nolan stopped and announced, "We're here."

She looked from side to side. The laneway was now nothing more than a thin path cutting through the center of one of the many orchards they passed. She laughed politely. "Well, you're 'here' does not appear to be anywhere," she concluded.

Nolan took a few steps toward the crumbling fence made of wood timbers providing a border along each side of the pathway. He placed the duffle bag he carried on the other side of the fence before putting his hands on the top beam. With a short leap, he propelled himself over the fence before turning himself back to Deahna, his hands held out to assist her. Deahna slid her narrow waist between his fingers. She took a small jump as his arms rose, setting her hips on the top beam. The light-green skirt rode up her thigh before the wind pushed it back down. Out of the corner of his eye, Nolan watched her swing her shapely legs over the rail, and he tugged on her waist, pulling her toward him. Her curved body slid down his as his hands caressed up her back.

Nolan placed a light kiss on her lips. Before she could purse her lips in response, he had already pulled away, leaving her with a confused look on her face. With a devilish grin, he stooped to pick up the bag and headed off into the orchard. He yelled back, "Come along! Just a little further!"

Her sandaled feet moved quickly to catch up while her eyes squinted in the sunlight as she hoped to see some sign of a final destination. Nolan kept up a good pace as they crested a hill, and in the shallow valley splayed out before them, a large pond filled the open space between the trees. There was a short wall of wood beams, five high, which dammed the far end of the pond and controlled the water level. Every time Nolan came here, he thought it was hard to believe this was a man-made overflow reservoir one thousand feet up on the platform of the city.

"This is gorgeous!" Deahna said as she stopped to let the vision sink into her memory.

A light breeze rippled the water. The comforting sound of the water's movement fit perfectly into the picturesque scene. Not many people came this way, and as a result, the grass, which had gone to seed, coated the shallow valley with a swaying coat of soft yellow. The orchard trees surrounding the pond displayed a dark-green canopy interrupted at random intervals by tight clusters of purple fruit. The meaty large melons, called surrels, were sweet, and the compact grouping of seeds only at the upper tip made the fruit easy to eat. Consequently, it was a favorite amongst the city folk of Bailemor.

After a few seconds, Deahna pointed to a tree next to the pond but not far from the dam. "Let's sit under that one," she proposed.

The tree Deahna referred to was unusual. In the wild it would have skyrocketed upward, but the farmers had placed curved metal rods along the saplings while they were still young and pliable. Forced back on themselves, the branches curved and twisted into an unusual configuration. Even the trunk, pressured by the rods, had displaced into a thick, bent form. The hand of nature, forever reaching outward, fought against the will of the farmers who kept the branches long and low for easier harvesting. Consequently, each tree resembled a great umbrella of green and purple, somehow teetering magically on its shaft. The tree they were now walking toward was at least 50 years old as were many others in the orchard. Ironically, the contorted limbs swaying lightly as the tips brushed the long grass, were breathtakingly beautiful.

Deahna bent low, slipping into the protected compartment made by the canopy. Kicking off her sandals, she said, "How ever did you find this place?"

Nolan pushed his way through the branches and let down the duffle bag. Squatting down, he unzipped it. "I saw this place from overhead on one of my training flights, at least a month ago. I was curious, so I came and explored it. The serenity is something I need from time to time." His eyes turned up to her. "It has been my little secret—one I've guarded carefully until now. I want to share it with you and make it *our* place."

"Well, I'm indeed honored." She lowered to her knees beside Nolan, curious as to the contents of the bag.

First, Nolan handed her a blanket to place on the grass, followed by another thinner satin sheet. Once set, Nolan began to pull out packed trays of food consisting of smoked meats, cheese and fruit. "On Earth this is what we call a country picnic," he said with a smile.

Deahna lay on her side, facing Nolan who had already slid down into a prone position on the blanket. They picked at the assortment of foods, spending as much time feeding each other as themselves. The sound of their laughter and light discussion meandered through the leaves between meaningless thoughts which were critical to the mood of the day. But that was about to change.

Deahna squeezed closer to Nolan. "Tell me about your Earth."

Nolan shrugged as he turned onto his back. "It's very different from this world, but in some ways, I think Crann Bith is what Earth will be centuries from now. Our planet is still alive, although my people strive to destroy its natural beauty. If only the people of my world, who still promote war, could come here and see the result. They might change their tune."

Leaning over him, she looked down into his face. "I thought you told me war was not predominant on Earth?"

"It's all relative," he responded. "We have our share of wars. They're smaller, shorter and less deadly than the ongoing epic war that seems to be part of your culture. Most areas of Earth are still safe and free of war. Here, war is everywhere and in everything."

"War is all I have ever known. My father died when I was eight. My mother is alive, but she is not well. The passing of her brother, then her husband, was too much for her. That in itself is sad, but what's even more sorrowful is, it's not a rare story. The war affects us all."

Nolan's brow furrowed. "Then why do you continue? Why can't you live in peace?"

"Don't get me wrong. My father died in the war. Six generations of men before him also died in the war." She paused. "I hate the war, but it's our way of life, and it's our survival. As purebloods, we've been gifted special powers. They're part of who we are as much as the war is now. There are very few naive people who think peace is an option."

"But there are a few. I've heard the rumors of a peace movement," he probed.

Deahna chuckled. "Very, very few. There has always been talk of a peace movement, but that is all it has been for centuries—just talk."

"Doesn't all the death bother you?"

Stretching her neck upward, Deahna looked out from under the canopy of leaves. Finding what she was looking for, she pointed to two small, black, bushy-tailed animals. "Do you see the two trailers over there?"

He propped up on an elbow, spying the two playful rodents. "Yes. They're similar to creatures we have on earth called squirrels."

"There are very few that die of old age," she said. "As it is with us all, man and animal alike, as we age our limbs become weak, our hearts falter and sometimes our minds wither. The trailers have an interesting twist. As their bodies begin to fail to a point where it's more a hindrance to the pack than a benefit, it begins to bloat. Its internal biology changes, and the creature grows fat to twice its size."

Nolan was having a difficult time following the line of discussion. "And your point is?"

"My point is, once the aged creature is good and fat, the others in the pack eat him. The old one, who is no longer a value to the pack, is sacrificed, and the pack continues to survive. The Celtae who die in the war also sacrifice themselves to the betterment of our race."

Nolan raised his voice a tone. "You have to be kidding. You're comparing human lives to rodents and talking of survival?"

"War and death are what we know."

"Then what of us, Deahna? Don't we have a future?" With those words, he saw the wall go up in her eyes, and a cold sterilized gaze came over them. She rolled over and stood, brushing the loose seed pods from her skirt. Moving over to the thick, angled tree trunk, she leaned back against it as the sole of her bare foot came up behind her to rest against the rough bark. She looked away into the thicket of leaves. "I don't know," she said with confusion in her eyes.

Nolan propped himself up on his arm. "Deahna, look at me," he said firmly.

Her face turned, the curls of her red hair bouncing as she shifted. Her green eyes looked down at him.

"I love you," he said as his voice became soft. He tried to hide the fact his eyes were moist.

She stared at him for several moments. Then her arm raised and she curled a finger to him. "Come here," she said with her voice barely above a whisper.

Rising, Nolan moved, leaning over her as she rested back against the tree trunk's slight angle. He could feel the warmth of her body as she lifted her face, kissing his upper lip, but it was different. Her teeth bit his lip, pulling back on it.

As she caressed her fingers along the back of his neck, she slid them up, tightening them into his hair. "I need you," she whispered. She furtively looked down as her other hand went to his shirt, undoing the buttons.

Nolan responded. His hand slid down her back, caressing her curves. Their bodies moved together as they undid the confines of the clothing enough so their hands could explore each other. He felt her calf slide up the back of his leg while his hands moved to support her. She responded eagerly, her other leg sliding up behind him. Her slender ankles locked around his waist, and her hand came to his cheek, pulling his eyes to hers. She wanted to see him at that moment as her body arched from their joining. Her lips parted, letting out a gasp. Then, her hand slid to the back of his neck, pulling his lips to her shoulder.

It was a delicate, sweet moment. Nolan buried his face into the crook between her neck and shoulder as he took her. He felt her body buck as his own passion flooded over him. *The moment was almost perfect,* he thought. *If only she had said those words—I love you too.*

Chapter 9

Julian flinched. He looked at the nostril hair he just yanked from his nose as if it was at fault. Shaking the tweezers in his hand, the hair fell into the bathroom sink alongside the others he pulled out before it. They stood out against the other longer, gray hairs he plucked from his ear canal at the beginning of the ordeal. Scrunching his face in one angle after the other, he inspected his nostril's image in the mirror. Tonight, he didn't need to look good. He needed to look perfect.

He walked through the door to the bedroom, lifting the jacket from the bed. A courier brought the new uniform yesterday, since he no longer wore the teal-blue of Watch Command. He was the first to wear the maroon uniform of the military with the added yellow collar, signifying him as a member of the *War Task Force*, or as it was simply dubbed—*WTF*. The five copper buttons on the collar were even more important, identifying his new rank of general.

Julian slid his arm into one sleeve, then the other as he walked to the full-length mirror across the room, hidden on the wall behind the entry door from the living room to the bedroom. He bounced his shoulders twice and turned his neck from side to side as he inspected his image. His lips formed a satisfied smile. He wouldn't look out of place at the dinner being held in his honor at the senator's house.

He was told it would be a small party with a total of 30 to 40 people. Just the upper echelon of the Kaezzar government was invited. He had been announced to his new position, but this would be the first time the senators would have an opportunity to meet him.

Julian nodded his head to his reflection. "Good evening," he said. "I am General Morenz." He gave a toothy smile and held his hand out.

"No…no…no," he muttered.

He straightened himself and snapped a salute. "Good to meet you, Senator," he chirped. "Hell no," he said, holding his chin as he contemplated the floor with his eyes.

He slouched, putting one hand into the pocket of his slacks. He half closed his eyes, bringing them back up to the mirror while giving a casual, tight-lipped smile. The other hand came up with a flick of his wrist, and his index finger swung forward. "I've heard so much about you, Senator," he said through a dry chuckle.

"No…no…no."

Pulling himself up straight, Julian cocked his head slightly to the left. *That's a good look*, he thought—*a deep, pondering life look*. Then, he smiled, but just barely. "Confident—very confident," he whispered. He slid his left hand out, his fingers forward, simulating a handshake, and after a moment, he closed his right hand on top of it. "Senator, I am humbled by the opportunity to support you."

Julian grinned wide as he clapped his hands together. "Oh, yes. You're the *god damn man!*" he snickered.

He spun on his left foot and walked away from the mirror. His neck was twisted as he looked behind himself, watching his reflection. Ten feet away, he turned and walked back toward the mirror, ensuring his pleats were still crisp. With a last smug grin, he walked through the doorway into the living room. His face changed into an open-mouthed scrunch as his finger and thumb were pulling at the back of his slacks. On his tip-toes, his back arched as he tried to get the underpants wedged up between his cheeks, out.

"Good afternoon, Captain Morenz, or should I say, General Morenz."

Julian's face contorted, and his legs instinctively threw him three feet until his back hit against the wall. "Who the hell…" He didn't finish the words. He squinted against the sunlight surrounding the man looking out his living room window. The shabbily dressed figure turned and returned the gaze.

"Peron, what are you doing here?" Julian looked anxiously from side to side before he walked to the window and shuffled the blinds closed.

Peron sauntered over to the living room couch, throwing himself back into the cushions. As his heels clicked onto the table in front of him, he said, "You hired me, and I have a report."

"Well, out with it then. What is so special about Nolan Harrison?"

Peron spoke slowly as he leaned his head back against the cushion. "I said I have a report. I didn't say it was the final report."

Although Julian was frustrated, he knew better than to push the spy. "I would appreciate the update then," he said.

"The man has done well since he arrived at Bailemor. He has powerful friends, and he has learned skills which will make it more difficult to finish this assignment." He drew out the last word, one syllable at a time. "I might well have to go beyond my normal bounds in getting the information you want."

"Five thousand more credits," Julian offered.

"That will help, but I'll need more than just money."

"I don't follow you. Speak up." An irritated edge came into Julian's voice.

Peron looked up with an elevated eyebrow. "With your new position, you will have the ability to command an Assault Squad. I will need one for a slight diversion."

"You're asking a lot."

Peron's scarred hand flew up, pointing a finger at Julian. "No," he said through clenched teeth. "*You* are asking a lot. You're not the one tip-toeing around a Celtae world. I am." His cold eyes stared Julian down.

"Okay, I get it. Relax, and tell me more. Why do you need this diversion?" Julian asked.

"Because someone is hiding something."

"That's not a surprise," Julian was quick to respond.

"I broke into the Crann Bith Immigration Center and pulled Harrison's file. A high-ranking official overruled the requirement to verify his DNA, and that's very strange."

Julian's eyebrows furrowed. "He's a Celtae, and his powers have been proven."

Peron rose to his feet. "I'm not sure what it means. Something doesn't add up, but it's more of a feeling I have." He smiled. "Sometimes you can have all the data in the world, but there's still the odd occasion when you have to go with that good old gut-feel."

Julian thought the smile made Peron look even more sinister. "You'll have your diversion when you need it." He turned and paced to the window to look out, unsure he was doing the right thing. He turned, and his lips opened to provide words of caution, but the living room was empty.

"I hate when he does that," Julian muttered.

He walked to the couch and sat down, avoiding the spot where Peron had just been sitting. He picked up his keyboard, activating the computer mode onto the video screen on the far wall. His fingers swept over the keys as he put in his password. The screen responded and was filled with the document he typed earlier in the morning. It was a request to transfer 38 personnel to his new staff. He spent a few days researching through classified files until he found the people who had the character he was seeking. The list was comprised of people who followed orders well. They were all smart, but none were brilliant. There were specialists in every category of espionage, including communications, infiltration, interrogation, explosives—the list was exhaustive. He hadn't shown his cards to Peron, but he already requested a five-member Assault Squad. Their names were near the bottom of the list.

Buried in the middle of the list was the name Jelan Tulis. He would have the requisition with him at dinner this evening, so he would keep his drinking light. On the other hand, the senator responsible for the war portfolio liked to have a good time, fueled by liberal amounts of alcohol. After a few drinks and some very patriotic discussion, Julian would find the right moment to spring the letter and pen toward him. It was unlikely he would even look at what he was signing.

Julian hit the print button with a boisterous flick of his finger. Again, he cocked his head to the side in a sympathetic pose and whispered, "Good evening. I'm General Morenz." *Yes*, he thought. *I have it all worked out.*

Chapter 10

It was stifling hot. This area of Crann Bith, just south of the equator, was swept by the warm winds coming from the mountains far to the west. These winds, having lost their moisture as they came off the leeward slopes, were dry, parching the land. Consequently, the landscape was a mix of sand and rock, spotted with a few short, fleshy trees having sharp spines in place of leaves. The landscape was desolate, but appropriate for the many Celtae having died this day.

Edwin looked out from his position amongst the few rocks flanking the battlefield. The day had not gone well. His brethren Celtae occupied the hard dune to his left. What had been 20 thousand soldiers two days ago, now could not number more than half that. The remainder were lifeless bodies, strewn across the sand between the Celtae's position and the Toltec front, several hundred yards to his right.

There was movement in the rear of the Toltec line as their cavalry swarmed before shooting out to make another foray against the Celtae left flank. There had been several such forays, focused on the left, trying to break down the line's organization.

Seeing the *Silver Riders*, called so because of the color of the plume on their helmets and their bright breast plates, the Celtae foot soldiers formed quickly into squares with their lances held outward to deter the Toltec charge. The Silver Riders accelerated across the gap. They rode trosks—large, thick-legged creatures that did well in these warmer climates. Their thin coat of wool-like hair kept them cooler than expected as they rumbled toward the Celtae line. Their menacing snarls added to the fury of the charge as their riders put spurs to their sides.

The Celtae squares shuffled closer together. Their shoulder-to-shoulder contact left no gaps in their line, but there was fear in their eyes as they saw the charge. The wild, yellow eyes of the trosks were a contrast to the deliberate, dark eyes of the Silver Riders looking out through the slits in their helmets.

Still 75 yards distant, the expected onslaught began. In unison the front row of riders pulled back their hands, then thrust them forward. At least 50 orange bursts of energy hurtled toward the Celtae squares. The Celtae bunched even closer while their individual energy shields combined into a large field of green, surrounding the square in its entirety.

Edwin cringed as he watched the orange bursts splatter into the Celtae. Sparks showered 30 yards in every direction as the Celtae square bent but did not fold. A few were knocked off their feet, but they quickly rose in time to see the second wave of orange bursts from the second row of riders, hurtling toward them. It was quickly followed by a third, then a fourth. With each, the green protective shield grew weaker.

A thundering crash careened across the battlefield as the front line of trosks all but leapt into the square. The first few were impaled on the steel-tipped lances, but those following snapped their jaws, adding to the death brought by the sword arms of the Silver Riders.

In each battle this is what it came to. The energy required to summon the orange bursts and to invoke the body shield of the Celtae, was not limitless. In fact, after three bursts, most Toltec were drained and unable to create another burst until they recouped their strength. This was also the case for the Celtae, whose energy shields would dissipate after absorbing a similar number of bursts. Edwin considered it a cruel balance of nature, keeping the two races evenly matched. Just as any would have predicted, it brought them, inevitably, to barbaric hand-to-hand combat.

The Celtae lancers fought valiantly, but Edwin could see it was only a matter of time before the sheer number of mounted riders overpowered the fewer Celtae. Edwin had tears in his eyes, understanding the sacrifice the soldiers of the left were making. Their names would go down in Celtae history as martyrs for their pureblood race.

He shook the mist from his eyes as the Celtae lancers broke. *A little too early*, he thought, but it would do. As expected, the Silver Riders followed. The Toltec leaders, seeing the broken line, ordered the infantry forward. Their commander, encouraged with the day's results, knew this was the time to put the final killing blow to the Celtae scourge. Throwing the majority of the infantry forward, they began a trot across the field toward the broken Celtae line with their swords thumping their shields in unison. The reverberating beat sent a shiver up Edwin's spine. It signaled their time to act.

Edwin, bent low, scurried back ten paces to the deep ravine cutting through the desert from north to south. He put his hand above his eyes to shield himself from the glint of two thousand helmets that filled the ravine as far as he could see. The Celtae cavalry, which was still supposed to be a day's ride from the battlefield, had ridden day and night to arrive in time to join the fight. They were weary, but the adrenaline would quickly bring them to life. This would be their moment in history.

Jumping off the lip of the ravine, Edwin landed on the saddle mounted to the back of his war trosk. He pulled on the helmet, adorned at the back with a light blue tie of hair, and raised his hand in a circling motion. As he whooped out the Celtae war cry, he kicked spurs to his trosk, compelling it to climb the side of the ravine and thrust out onto the arid plain.

As they charged, the middle of the line moved faster than the two ends. It was a precise move resulting in a pointed front, ready to cut through any and all standing before them. Edwin saw a few Toltec heads turn and yell out, but the din of the battle drowned out their voices. In any case, since the Toltec infantry was committed at the Celtae front, it would be difficult for them to withdraw considering they were fully engaged. The Silver Riders were on the other side of the infantry, and although they were trying to come about to face the charging Celtae cavalry, their own infantry was impeding them.

The flying, arrow-shaped charge split into two as they came across the Toltec rear. Half went east to plough into what remained of the Toltec reserves, while Edwin led the charge into the rear of the unsuspecting infantry. Edwin's sword came down time and again into the flesh of the enemy as his trosk trampled through the fallen bodies. The leaders of the Toltec infantry, finally realizing their predicament, tried to turn their army and retreat back to their lines, but they were caught between Edwin's riders and the renewed charge of the Celtae main line. The battle was now a slaughter, as the bulk of the Toltec infantry were caught between the Celtae pincers. There was no mercy asked for, and no quarter was given.

Edwin saw the last small group of surviving Silver Riders trying to force their way back to their lines to the south. He motioned to his men, and ten came with him to cut off the Rider's retreat. The eyes of the Silver Rider's leader met Edwin's. No words were required as they both tugged the reins, pressing their mounts to a gallop toward each other.

As the two beasts crossed paths, the teeth of Edwin's trosk flashed a bite into the flank of the Silver Rider's beast. At the same moment, Edwin's sword clashed with the other man's, and the orange sparks from the steel-to-steel contact was lost in the clamor of the battle. Edwin reared up his beast, compelling it to turn just in time to face the Silver Rider whose sword was already swinging down toward him. Edwin deflected the blow as the

Silver Rider took the offensive, slashing and swinging his sword in a furious but controlled attack. He saw the fury in the Silver Rider's eyes as the man knew the battle was lost. The thought of the Celtae turning the tide and winning the day, played on the Silver Rider's mind. It was only a matter of time before he would lose focus and make a fatal mistake.

It didn't take long for the opening to come. The Silver Rider just completed a back-handed strike that was deflected by Edwin's sword, when the rider tried to turn his trosk into Edwin's. Edwin saw it coming and swung his own trosk to his left as his sword came slashing across in a horizontal sweep. The silver Rider was off balance, having turned too far, and his sword arm was too far from Edwin to block the slash of whirling steel. The tip of Edwin's sword creased across the front of the Silver Rider's neck, cutting a neat, thin line through his flesh.

Blood began to pool at the cut as the Silver Rider's eyes went wide. He knew he would be dead in a few seconds. He gurgled. Blood choked his gasps for air. As the Silver Rider toppled from his mount, Edwin felt a sharp pain in his side. He lurched, looking down to see the infantryman who just stabbed him with a spear. The Toltec warrior screamed out, as he was quickly cut down by one of Edwin's fellow riders, but it was too late. The blow had fallen, and it would be fatal.

Edwin knew what the Silver Rider did. He would be dead in a few moments. The blood was pumping from the wound under his arm the way it did when a vital organ was hit. He felt hands pulling him to the ground. His fellow riders formed a circle around him as he lay in the arms of two of his men who knelt on the blood-soaked ground. Edwin tried to speak, but blood filled his mouth and his breathing was difficult. He saw the tears in the eyes of his men—the men he would miss dearly. With great effort, Edwin raised his arm and pointed westward. Barely above a whisper, his voice came to him for his last words. "Let me see."

His men parted the circle so Edwin could see through the line where the fighting had all but stopped. At the far end of the field, littered with dead bodies, a sole Celtae was raising a pike. He had found a Celtae flag torn almost in two, and speared it with the point of the pike. He dug the blunt end into the sand so the flag fluttered in the dry breeze against the red sun setting in the background. As the men turned back to look at Edwin, he was motionless. Death had taken him. He died a hero and was forever known as the famed Desert Rider of Crann Bith.

A soft tune began to play through the theatre's speakers as the picture on the movie screen faded into black. Lukas looked at Nolan seated in the chair next to him, and between mouthfuls of nuts, said, "So, what did you think?"

Nolan looked at his friend and shrugged. "As a movie, I've seen better, but that's not a surprise to me. On Earth making movies is a big business. In fact, on my world entertainment is almost as big an industry as the effort here toward the war."

"Every world has its heroes and villains," Lukas replied. "I was told the movie was accurate in its detail."

"I have to think the movie might have a slightly altered storyline from reality," Nolan offered. "Let's face it. The battle was over 300 years ago, and the producers have a commitment to tell a true story. It's almost as strong as their incentive to tell the viewers what they want to hear. I don't think the movie would be as popular if Edwin died screaming in pain, begging for someone to put him out of his misery. That's a more probable ending."

Raising an eyebrow, Lukas said, "You're becoming very cynical."

"I would think, long ago, many of the purebloods must have felt the same, but cynicism takes effort, and after a time, I'm sure they felt it was wasted," Nolan surmised.

Lukas, having finished his nuts, wiped his fingers on a napkin. "I need to go. I'm going out tonight with Jersey. Are you sure you don't want to join us? We're going to the *Tidewater*. It's a new club. The music is supposed to be great, and from what I've heard, a real draw for pretty women."

Nolan chuckled as his hand slapped down on Lukas's shoulder, and then he used the same hand to push himself out of the chair. "You know I'm committed. Besides, I'm meeting Daniel for dinner this evening."

"To each his own," Lukas answered. "But I think I'll be in better company—more attractive at any rate," he said as he rose to his feet.

The two men made their way out the exit while long shadows from the late afternoon sun mottled the avenue in front of the theatre. They veered left toward the parking garage where the borrowed bullet car was stored.

As they walked, Lukas watched the bouncing shoulders of his shadow on the sidewalk. He focused there as he told Nolan the news he had been dreading to divulge. "I've taken an assignment," he said. His face looked up, squinting as the sunlight bounced off a tall, glass-covered building in front of them.

"That's great!" Nolan said as he turned toward Lukas. But when he saw

Lukas's stoic face, he knew there was something unsettling in his blue-haired friend's announcement. He tried to hold the smile, waiting for Lukas to continue.

"I have joined the *Dreadmen*. I think their spirit best fits my personality."

Nolan knew there was good and bad in Lukas's words. The Dreadmen were an elite military squad. The best way to describe their specialty was to say they were trained to be brave. They took the missions other divisions turned down. Missions thought to have impossible odds, but nevertheless needing to be attempted, were given to the Dreadmen. The title in itself spoke much of the assignment. The Dreadmen were ice-cold experts in life and death and knew how to sustain themselves in the most inhospitable environments. The skill was matched by the numerous ways they could efficiently bring death to their targets when called upon. They were a results-based group held in awe by the people of Crann Bith as mysterious heroes of the war effort.

"Congratulations, Lukas. There are very few the Dreadmen consider worthy to be in their group. You must have made quite an impression." Nolan kept his tone cheerful, thinking of the positive side of the appointment.

"It was a difficult decision, but after struggling with it, I felt it was where I belonged—at least for as long as I'm able to serve with them."

Nolan heard Lukas's words and knew what his friend meant. The Dreadmen were sometimes mockingly referred to as the *Deadmen*. For just as acceptance automatically brought the title of *hero*, so did it typically bring an early grave. Nolan also read between the lines. He knew the Dreadmen were a secretive group, spending most of their time sequestered or on a mission. Sometimes the missions could be long-term reconnaissance affairs, literally lasting years. "When do you go?" Nolan asked.

"In one week. After that, you might not see much of me."

They had reached the stairs going down to the parking garage. At the bottom, Nolan turned to Lukas and clasped his arm. "No matter where you are, I'll remember we are bond brothers. When your voice calls, mine will answer. No decisions required. It will be so."

Lukas responded, "Although it might be more difficult for me, I'll make the same oath. In fact, I made such when I became your bond brother. I have an allegiance to the Dreadmen, but my oath is to you. It shall always be in that order."

After giving Lukas a ride to his quarters, it took Nolan another 20 minutes to arrive back at Daniel's home. As he swung open the door, he called out, but there was no response. Both Germaine and Daniel were out. Nolan's face vibrated in a wide yawn as he realized he was weary. He still had an hour before he had to leave to meet Daniel for dinner. His steps took him to his bedroom where he threw himself back on the bed, hoping to utilize the hour for sleep.

However, it was not to be. His thoughts were still on Lukas and the dangerous position he had accepted with the Dreadmen. On one hand, he felt slighted. Lukas hadn't told him about the position until after he'd accepted it, but then Lukas was headstrong and his own man in every way. Nolan respected the fact it was a decision Lukas felt he had to make by himself.

The thoughts didn't take long to change focus onto himself. He had been on Crann Bith for six months now and had finished the Academy with honors. He spent time with Deahna who he loved deeply, and in many respects, he was fitting into Bailemorian society, but something was missing. He had no purpose, no goals, and without goals there were no successes—the successes required to justify one's life.

He had discussed the issue with Daniel, and of course the older man had recommended patience. That discussion quickly turned into a focus on the Soichaint, and here, Daniel used all his expertise in confusing Nolan with riddles. Daniel told him of his importance to the effort but was vague in the details. Nolan was frustrated and even lashed out at Daniel, asking, "If he was so important, why were his skills not being utilized?" The older man scolded him, telling Nolan, now was the time for him to continue to practice his skills, so when the time came the Soichaint could depend on him.

Begrudgingly, Nolan complied. He still went to the Academy to practice and improve his abilities. He sparred with the sensei, by now giving as many blows as he took. His psychic abilities were also continuing to improve to a fine-tuned level. He knew the power of his shield and his ability to manipulate his mind within the Athar were both reaching an expert level. Often, at night, he would float his mind through the Athar, peeking into different planes. It was a contrast to his first dream where he had ripped open the energy expanse. Now, he could slide in without almost a trace of a wake.

The only aspect of his abilities that was troubling came when he invoked his shield, when he would continually feel a tingling in his fingertips as his mind focused on the energy field. He learned to override the sense and could quickly surround himself with the green energy field at will, but it still bothered him almost like a slight stammer in someone's speech. When he discussed it with Daniel, he told Nolan it was a minor issue and something he should not worry about.

Through the closed door, Nolan heard the front door being opened. Finally, giving in to his uncooperative conscious mind, he arose and moved toward the living area. Turning the corner from the hallway, he saw Germaine placing a few grocery bags onto the table in the kitchen area.

Germaine smiled a greeting. "I'm surprised you're still here. You'll be late for dinner with Daniel."

Nolan pulled his arm up and looked at his watch. "No, it'll take 30 minutes, at the most, to get to the Green Mountain Restaurant."

Germaine raised an eyebrow, giving Nolan a quizzical look. "The Green Mountain Restaurant—that's not right. Daniel is going to meet you at the Wooden Rail Pub. That's at least another 20 minutes further away, across the bridge on the Gwynedd Peak."

"Why on Earth, or for that matter on Crann Bith, would Daniel go to the Wooden Rail Pub?" Nolan replied with his hands planted on his hips and a confused look on his face.

Germaine gave a scoffing laugh. "Where is your mind, Nolan? You called this morning, and you left a message for Daniel on the computer comm. You said your plans changed, and you would meet him at the Wooden Rail."

Nolan's gaze turned stone-cold. "I never made that call."

"I was here when it came in," Germaine said under his breath, thinking back to the morning.

There was an unsettling pause. "Daniel's in danger," Nolan said before he hastened to the storage closet by the front door.

Germaine's face went dark, foreboding evident in his eyes, as he came to the same realization.

Nolan threw open the door to the storage closet. He took out a knife and put it in the sheath attached to the left side of his belt. He reached his hand in, pulling out the second belt and scabbard holding the curved sword. He slung the belt over his shoulder, securing the clasp along his chest. As he pulled on his jacket overtop the weapons, tying the belt into a knot, he turned to Germaine. "Do you know where the Wooden Rail Pub is?"

Germaine nodded his affirmation.

"Good." Nolan's voice was crisp and carried an assertive edge. "I'm going there as quickly as I can. Lukas and Jersey are at the new Tidewater Club." He pointed his finger at Germaine. "Go there and get them. Bring them to the Wooden Rail. Daniel is going to need our help."

Without waiting for a reply, Nolan was already out the door as it swung shut behind him. It took only minutes for him to arrive at the bullet car and type in the fastest possible monorail route to the bridge. Once there, he changed lines, redirecting the bullet across one of the rails suspended from the bridge's structure. Having only been on the Gwynedd Peak once before, he needed to rely on the bullet car's navigation link to guide him the rest of the way to the parking complex nearest the row of buildings housing the pub.

Nolan stepped from the stairwell out onto street level that was dark except for the streetlight's dim glow every 30 yards. He stopped momentarily, getting his bearings while trying not to look conspicuous. As he panned his eyes from side to side, he realized this was a seedy part of the city. Even in the low light level, he could see the sidewalks were cracked, and the buildings were dirt-covered. Only a few people were walking at street level, and more than once Nolan saw them nervously look behind themselves as they walked at a quick pace.

Ahead, not 50 yards from the stairwell, Nolan saw a yellow-lit sign, framed in wood with black letters. It read - *The Wooden Rail Pub*. Keeping his hands limber and at the ready, he walked quickly toward the sign, sighting down each narrow alley separating the buildings he passed. Once at the pub, he stayed in the shadows, slowly edging his face to the side until he could see in the corner of the wide pane of glass.

Nolan was surprised the interior of the restaurant looked warm and inviting. Almost everything within was made of wood, varnished to a dark, rich sheen. Ornate wrought-iron lights hung from the ceiling at several locations, casting shadows across the stained-glass dividers separating each booth. Only one of the ten booths was occupied. He also observed there was a man cleaning glasses behind the bar and one waiter who just passed through the swinging door leading to the kitchen.

Pulling his face away from the window, Nolan furtively looked up and down the narrow street. There was no sign of Germaine yet. He should wait, but his sixth sense was screaming at him. *Daniel was in danger!* He made a decision and pressed open the door of the pub.

As he entered, the man behind the bar nodded, pointing to the tables on the left. "We're not very busy tonight. Pick a booth and Des will be right with you."

Nolan walked to the third booth. He heard a raspy noise from below and looked down to see the floorboards covered with a thin layer of wood chips. Although the wood chips gave the elegant restaurant a down-home feel, it was the woodsy scent that added to the atmosphere. From the booth, he could get a good view of all the seating areas. He loosened the knot in his belt, but didn't remove his jacket. Since the city was at war, it was not uncommon to wear weapons, but it would be unwise to bring any undue attention, especially to an Akkadian in the Gwynedd portion of Bailemor.

The door from the kitchen swung open and Des made his way to Nolan. The waiter was middle-aged, balding with a small pot belly—unusual on Bailemor as the scientists long ago developed drugs to control obesity.

Des placed a menu on the table. "What can I get you?"

Nolan picked it up, strumming the pages with his thumb. His gray eyes turned up to the portly man. "I'm looking for someone—an Akkadian who I was supposed to meet here. He's older, thin-boned with blonde hair and a blonde, bushy moustache. Have you seen such a person here tonight?"

"No, can't say that I have," Des promptly replied, placing his hands on his hips.

Nolan thought the answer came much too quickly. He opened the menu, looking through it. "You're sure?"

"Of course. I've been here all night," Des said in an irritated tone.

"Just a cold glass of beer to quench my thirst, then." Nolan closed the menu and placed it flat on the table. With two fingers, he slid it to the edge, where Des picked it up.

"A cold glass of beer, right away," Des said just before walking to the bar.

Nolan's eyes scanned every crevice of the restaurant. Something wasn't right. Des was on edge, and even now, Nolan could see in his peripheral vision that the man behind the bar continually glanced toward him as he whispered to Des. Des came back to the booth with the beer, sidestepping the people from the other booth who were now leaving. He placed the drink on the table while Nolan pulled two coins from his pocket and slid them across the table to the waiter.

"Will there be anything else?" Des asked as he pocketed the coins.

Nolan took a long drink from the tall glass, then smiled up to Des. "No, that'll be all. Thanks."

Des went to the kitchen area through the swinging door after again casually dropping a whisper to the man behind the bar. Nolan brought the cool drink to his lips, then glanced at his watch. Germaine was taking too long. The man behind the bar went into the kitchen area, and Nolan tried to focus on the voices. They were too low for him to make out the words, but he could discern at least three different tones. There was at least one other man in the kitchen besides the two he had seen thus far.

Des and the bartender came out from the kitchen just as Nolan arose after finishing his drink. He nodded to the men and then turned before stepping out the front door onto the sidewalk where, to his right, he saw three dark figures walking briskly toward him. He exhaled with relief when the first figure moved under a street light, revealing himself as Germaine. Nolan trotted over to them and pulled them into the shadows of the building.

Nolan whispered, "Daniel's in there."

"Then why did he not come out with you?" Germaine asked while carrying a look of confusion on his face.

Nolan shook his head from side to side. "No—no—he was there in the restaurant, and I believe he's still in the back, but he's not in the public area. Something isn't freaking right."

"How do you know?" Lukas's face became visible, as he stepped out from behind Jersey.

"Three things. The remains of a dinner roll were still on a plate in a booth which had not been cleaned up. The bun was eaten all the way around in neat circles, and Daniel can be the only person on any plane who does that. I also noticed there were unusual markings in the wood chips on the floor. It would appear someone was dragged into the kitchen. The third thing is the feeling I have in my gut. He's there."

"Then what are we waiting for?" Germaine asked as he pulled a long knife from under his coat.

Nolan laid his hand on Germaine's. "Let's keep it simple. We're in Gwynedd territory, and it might not be the wisest course of action for four Akkadians to spill Gwynedd blood on their ground."

Germaine nodded and sheathed the knife. "What's the plan?"

"There are at least three men in the pub. One will be behind the bar. The other two could be in the kitchen or the serving area. "Germaine—" Nolan pressed his finger into the warrior's chest "—you will enter first. Take out the man behind the bar. Just be careful. The way his hands were fidgeting earlier, I think he has a weapon behind the counter. I'll follow you, but I will veer right and head straight into the kitchen. If the waiter is in my way, I'll take him out." He turned to Lukas and Jersey. "I'm sure there is a back door. Take the alley and find it. Wait outside until you hear me within, and then get in. I don't really care how. Find a way." He looked from man to man. "Understood?"

All three nodded.

"Good, "Nolan said. "Be careful, all of you." He slapped Lukas on the shoulder. "We'll give you two minutes to get to the back door."

The two men scooted down the side alley leading them to the back of the row of buildings. Nolan and Germaine kept to the shadows as they moved toward the front of the pub. Nolan turned his head back and forth. There was no one else on the street. It was deserted except for the two of them. Germaine put his hand on the door handle as Nolan placed his hand on Germaine's shoulder.

Nolan took one last look up and down the street and yelled, "Now!"

The door burst open. It took only three running strides for Germaine to be up to speed. He launched himself over the bar and tumbled into the man, forcing a wide-eyed look of surprise on his face as the energy pistol tumbled from his grasp.

Nolan veered to the right, thumping into the swinging door to the kitchen. As it burst off its hinges, he saw Des leaning over an unconscious Daniel who was spread across some larger boxes. Nolan altered his direction, letting his momentum carry him into the man, pasting him against the wall. He heard the wind expel from Des's lungs as he slumped to the ground. Curled into a ball, the man gasped for air.

Nolan turned quickly, coming face to face with another man who was just pulling a pistol from the holster at his belt. As Nolan instantly invoked his energy shield, the window crashed open behind the man. The blue-haired, wild-eyed figure of Lukas flew through the window and tumbled into the Gwyneddman, sending the gun sliding in circles across the wooden floor. It only took Lukas one blow to dispatch the third man who fell unconscious to the floor. The back door burst open, as Jersey knocked his shoulder against it. He looked quickly from side to side, his fists clenched, looking for any further Gwyneddman to dispatch.

Nolan turned to his friends just as Germaine came through the remnants of the door frame. "I think we have all of them," Nolan said through deep breaths.

Germaine nodded assertively. "Indeed, none are left standing."

Nolan leaned over Daniel while his fingers moved to the older man's neck. He lifted one of his eyelids and then the other. "Thank god. He's just unconscious."

Germaine, looking over Nolan's shoulder, added, "I think from the look of his eyes, he's been drugged."

There was a creak from the back of the kitchen. As Nolan lifted his head, he saw a figure shift from behind a row of shelves and fly out the back doorway.

"Dragon!" Nolan hissed.

The Earthman flew to the door and caught himself with his fingers as he grasped the door jamb. He looked back at his friends. "Get Daniel home. This is my fight." The last words were lost in the distance, as he was already running down the back alley after the Gwyneddman.

The alley was devoid of lights, but fortunately, the moon peeked out from behind the clouds, allowing him to see Dragon ahead, running with all haste. The dark-haired Gwyneddman disappeared down a side alley away from the street as Nolan recklessly followed, grasping the wooden corner trim on the building. It helped turn his body without losing speed. Dragon was closer. He saw the man look back before turning left down another of the many crisscrossed side alleys. Nolan's mouth was open, deep panting breaths being drawn into lungs, feeling as if they would burst. Once again, his left hand reached out to hold the corner of the building, allowing him to swing around it at full speed.

He didn't see the fist, but he felt it. Dragon's knuckles slammed into his cheek, stopping his upper body at that point. His lower body continued forward causing his legs to swing wildly out from under him. He did a backward somersault, finally landing on his stomach. His forehead bounced on the bricks surfacing the back alley, and Nolan could feel the trickle of blood from his brow.

Dragon, several feet away, looked down at Nolan whose chest was heaving as he gasped for air. The back of Nolan's jacket had ripped as he fell, revealing the sword. In an instant, Dragon reached behind him, pulling out his own three-foot length of steel.

The recognizable sound of Dragon's sword being drawn brought Nolan's mind back into focus. He turned, got to his knees, then his body swayed as he struggled to gain his feet. Finally righting himself, he leaned over while placing one hand on each knee. "I never came here for a sword fight. I ran after you to knock some sense into you," Nolan said.

Dragon's eyes were wide. "Your words do not match your actions!" He lifted his hand, jerking the sharp tip of his blade toward the sword in the scabbard along Nolan's back.

With some difficulty, Nolan stood upright. "I don't mean to kill you just to…" He had to jump backward to avoid the slash from Dragon's sword. Having no choice, he quickly slid his own sword from the sheath. He faced Dragon, at the ready. "As you wish then. No more words," he said with his eyes ablaze.

The two men circled each other as lights began to illuminate rooms in the second story of the buildings backing onto the dark alley. Shutters were thrust open, inquisitive faces leaned over for a better view while others were more careful, peeking through the cracks.

In one way, Nolan was relieved to see the people watching. It would ensure the fight was fought fairly, but on the other hand, the eyes might bring more Gwynedd warriors to Dragon's aid, and that was a concern if the fight was prolonged. Nolan refocused on Dragon who shimmied toward him, unleashing a series of overhand strokes. He ducked just in time as the last stroke, in a sweeping side arc, hit into the bricks of the building, showering sparks into the dark of night. Nimbly, Nolan pushed off the wall and turned while his own arm came around in a sweep. Dragon turned just as quickly, deflecting the blow.

Realizing he was in a weak position with his back to the wall, Dragon shifted forward again with a flurry of thrusts. Nolan parried each. Dragon's last thrust was knocked downward by Nolan as he side-stepped in toward the Gwynedd general's son. There, the Earthman brought his elbow, in a back-handed blow, to the Gwyneddman's chin.

Dragon staggered a step back, shaking his head. Carefully, he circled. Nolan shifted his feet, keeping outside of the reach from Dragon's sword arm. Seeing his advantage, Nolan took the offensive. Subtle flicks of his wrist brought the sword, time and again, toward Dragon's body. He worked toward the left side of Dragon's body, then suddenly adjusted his wrist, propelling a thrust toward the right side of Dragon's chest—but it was a feint. Nolan pulled back his hand, and the sword came toward Dragon's left side in a powerful, tight circle.

Dragon reacted. His sword arm would not make it back in time. Instinctively, his energy shield flared around his body just in time to deflect the damaging blow. There were shouts from the people who watched from the second-floor windows.

Nolan stepped back, feeling the numbness in his wrist as if he had punched a wall. He knew the code for duels. Celtae had a way to put the shield to the back of their subconscious mind for fixed periods of time. Nolan had done so, but apparently Dragon had not. This changed the Earthman's perspective. In this duel, he was hoping not to be killed, but at the same time, he hoped to give the Gwyneddman only an educational wound. That would be difficult with the less than moral advantage Dragon held.

Slowly, Nolan brought his sword up. The blazing anger was gone from his eyes, replaced with determination and a cold gray to match the shade of his sword's steel. He said, "Now you need to beware."

Dragon smirked. Then he flung himself at Nolan. Two blows rung off the outside of Nolan's sword as the Earthman backed away. Nolan let Dragon press him back into the length of the alley. Nolan deflected blow after blow. With each, Dragon became more reckless in his assault as his mind focused on the offensive blows. Dragon thrust forward wildly. Nolan sidestepped to the left as the sword skimmed his chest. Before Dragon could regain his balance, Nolan pressed his sword across his body, into the Gwyneddman's side.

Dragon staggered back with his mouth gaping open as a trickle of blood dripped from the corner of his lips. He slid off the sword, falling to his knees. Dropping his own sword, he put his hand to the wound in a futile effort to stem the flow of blood. He looked to the wound before raising his eyes to Nolan. The eyes glazed over and became lifeless as Dragon's hands fell from the wound. Finally, his body tumbled onto the brick alleyway.

With the sound of clashing steel now past, people came out of the doors backing onto the alley to look upon Dragon's body. Nolan peered up the narrow lane, as he heard distant feet hitting the bricks in a run toward him. Several men were coming.

He heard his name yelled from the side alley. "Nolan—this way!" Nolan turned to see a man in the shadows, his back pressed against the wall. He couldn't mistake the shock of blue hair. Through clenched teeth, Lukas said, "We have to get out of here!"

Nolan didn't waste any time. He sheathed his sword, then ran after Lukas into the darkness of the alley, away from the death he left behind.

Just as their footfalls receded into the night, three young Gwyneddmen came running from the opposite end of the alley. One of them said, through panting breaths, "We heard there was a duel—" His chest was heaving "—between a Gwyneddman and an Akkadian."

A second Gwyneddman bent down over the lifeless body. "It's Dragon Treve!" He looked up at the first Gwyneddman. "He's dead—murdered."

A voice echoed down from an upper window. "It was no murder, but a fair fight, at least on the part of the Akkadian!"

There were murmurs of agreement in the growing crowd.

The first Gwyneddman turned to the growing cluster of onlookers. "This is the son of General Treve. The general will need an accounting of what transpired this night. Who will come forward?"

The crowd shrank back, all except one dark figure cloaked in black. The cloaked man spoke slowly. "I was here from the start. I'll tell General Treve what happened." Peron lifted his scarred hand, pulling the pipe from his lips. He turned it over, dumping the burnt concoction of exotic herbs onto the alleyway where it mixed with the dark Gwynedd blood seeping into the bricks.

Chapter 11

With one hand on either side of Deahna's shoulders, Nolan pushed up and rolled off her onto his back. As he wiped the beads of perspiration from his brow, she turned on her side, nuzzling her chin into the crook between his arm and shoulder. Her smooth-skinned leg came up across his thighs and her heel locked against the far side of his calf.

As always, their lovemaking was both energetic and deeply passionate. They lay naked, clutched together for quite some time without any words to spoil the sweet moment—one that should have been clear of thoughts of the outside world.

Nolan looked up at the ceiling of the whitewashed hut at the top of the cliffs, two hundred yards above the beach. The long-abandoned structure, built into the craggy juts of white rock dotting the steep hillside, was from a by-gone day. The wooden timbers supporting the roof were cracked and pitted, but their rigid girth foretold they would hold for tens of years yet to come. Nolan and Deahna had snuck away to the seclusion of the hut, leaving Lukas and the rest of the former cadet squad on the long, curved sandy beach at the base of the cliff. For two hours the hut had provided an escape from the war, from the bustle of the city and even from their friends who came with them on this tropical weekend getaway.

Deahna broke the silence with a chuckle. "Crann Bith to Nolan. Crann Bith to Nolan."

He looked down into her smiling green eyes and laughed. "Yes, my mind is moving a mile a minute." It was this way quite often. As much as he wanted his thoughts to be calm, they always quickly moved to the many deep concerns he had.

"You still have Dragon on your mind?"

Nolan exhaled with a deep sigh. "Yes. I know, in part, his death was my fault."

Deahna's fingers slid across his chest, playing with the thin layer of hair, but she remained silent.

Chuckling, Nolan said, "Isn't this where you say, 'You shouldn't harbor guilt since there was nothing you could've done differently.'" He looked thoughtfully at the ceiling as his fingers caressed Deahna's shoulder. "Back on Earth, in the movies, it never ended like this. There, when the villain is killed, it's always accidental—some type of unavoidable slip causing the foe to die, leaving the hero remorseful but at the same time blameless. When Dragon ran, I could've let him go, but I chose to follow him. Even once the fight was engaged, I could've laid down my sword and submitted."

Deahna turned onto her stomach, leaning her chin on her palm as her elbow perched on Nolan's chest. "You're right. Things could have been handled differently, but they weren't. You made split-second decisions to save both Daniel and yourself. Dragon had been pestering and goading you for some time. If he had let it go, he would be alive today. The judge in the hearing saw it the same way. He ruled there were no grounds to proceed with any charges against you, so you're innocent of any wrongdoing."

Nolan looked up into her green eyes. "But I lost control twice, both when I chased after him, and when we were in the sword fight. I wanted to kill him, and now he's dead. I thought I was better than that."

Her hand came across to stroke his cheek. "You are a wonderful man, Nolan, and you have strong, deeply imbedded emotions. If you didn't, you wouldn't be human."

Nolan brought his hand up to cover hers. "General Treve might not agree with you. Apparently, he was incensed at the decision of the judge at the inquiry. Rumor has it he's sworn vengeance and is set to continue the harassment his son began. In a way, I agree with him. I know Dragon began the fight, but I finished it with a little too much gusto. So, forgive me if I don't agree with you. Right now, I don't like the person I am."

Deahna slid up with her full breasts dragging along Nolan's chest. She tilted her head down once, placing a soft kiss on his lips, then another. Her face was only a breath away from his as she looked into his gray eyes. Her voice came like a soft flow of spring air. "Some things have been difficult for me to accept. It's not even a realization, but more of an admission. I knew a long time ago my feelings for you went far beyond 'like.' I've been afraid to admit it, but I do love you Nolan Harrison—with all my heart and soul."

Moments like this gave meaning to life. She finally opened up to him, pulling down the walls that had kept her feelings locked in. What had been in her heart for months, finally spilled from her lips. Nolan returned the gaze and looked through her eyes deep into her soul. He saw her beauty deeper than her physical appearance, and there was no reason to add words to the moment. Everything he needed to say was said with the look of deep love held in his eyes.

The serenity was interrupted by yelling from the beach below amidst the sound of sporadic electrical discharges.

Nolan's eyes went wide. "That's laser rifle fire!" he cried as he pushed Deahna to the side. Jumping to his feet, three quick steps took him to the glassless window opening where he carefully peered out to the beach below.

There, he saw Jersey, shrouded within his green energy shield, overturn a large, wooden beach table for cover. Lukas was five yards in front of him, crouched over, walking backward. He was pulling the smoldering form of Jennee toward the cover Jersey was putting in place. A blue energy burst thudded into Lukas's energy shield. In a shower of sparks, he was thrown back, landing sprawled on his back. The blue-haired man was dazed, but he still had enough sense to crawl behind the cover where Jersey was pinned down.

Nolan was immediately concerned about Jennee. At first, he thought she was dead, but her arms were moving in an effort to drag herself out of the crossfire. Her movements were very slow, and Nolan knew she was badly injured.

From his elevated vantage point, Nolan could see four assailants in the rocks at the bottom edge of the cliff. They gave continuous fire toward the cover Lukas and Jersey had taken. Each time a blue laser burst would fly across the sand and hit into the wood, it would leave a black patch and wisps of smoke from the release of energy. Lukas and Jersey managed to recover their laser pistols and were returning the fire as best they could through the openings between the gaps in the beach furniture they had hastily erected as a barrier.

An alarm could be heard sounding in the distance as Deahna now stood beside him, naked except for the blanket she had draped around herself. "Who are they, Toltec or Anasazi?" she asked.

"I would think they are Toltec," Nolan replied. He hastily turned and pulled on his shorts, tank top and sandals. He grasped the laser pistol he had been assigned once they arrived at the resort world and checked to see it was fully charged. On the beach, the laser battle was a stalemate. Off in the distance, he could see two speedy patrol boats racing toward them, throwing up a white wash as the bows broke the green salt water. "I'm going to wait here. I don't want to leave you alone," he said to Deahna.

Deahna saw the way Nolan nervously fingered the pistol. She stood on her tiptoes to get a better view. Jennee had stopped moving. She needed medical attention immediately, if in fact she was still alive. Out of the corner of her eye, she saw a movement against the white rocks of the cliff. She pointed her finger toward it. "Look there!"

Nolan followed the direction of her finger. Halfway down the cliff, crouched amongst the rocks, a fifth assailant was making his way unseen into a position which would flank Lukas and Jersey. In a few minutes, he would be able to fire around the wooden barricade into Nolan's unsuspecting friends. Several times, Nolan looked from the oncoming boats to the man, trying to avoid a difficult decision.

Finally, Nolan turned to Deahna. "Stay here. I need to help them. The boats won't make it in time."

She nodded her head as Nolan kissed her, then he raced out the door.

Quietly, Nolan slid his way down through the rocks. He needed to be closer to obtain a clear, accurate shot. He would only have one opportunity, and if he missed or even just injured the man, the more powerful laser rifle would make short work of him. He was also wary not to energize his shield yet. It might draw attention to him, and he needed the element of surprise for the fifth assailant. Every few seconds he looked up, seeing the boats coming ever closer, but the man was almost in position. Making very little noise, Nolan scooted down between the white rocks, and as the man raised his rifle toward an unsuspecting Lukas and Jersey, Nolan jumped out into the open, firing one blast from his pistol. There was a pulsing, electrical sound just before the blue energy burst hit the man squarely in the back of his head. The impact pushed him forward, his body pitching several yards down the cliff. In his final seconds of life, a flicker of orange energy sputtered about his fingers but quickly dissipated as he tumbled down the steep cliffside.

The other four men on the beach saw their comrade's body fall as energy bursts from the oncoming boats were now hitting into the surf just short of the beach. Nolan rushed down to the sand to see the four men become obscured by the rippling ovals created by their transposition. As the beach was flooded with intensified fire from the boat's laser cannons, the four men vanished, successfully hopping out before the rein of cannon fire consumed them.

The two boats shot up on the beach as a dozen heavily armed soldiers jumped down onto the sand. Half went in each direction along the shoreline to secure their position. Lukas and Jersey were joined by Nolan at the burnt figure of Jennee. Lukas turned her over and felt for a pulse. He looked up and shook his head from side to side. She was gone.

As Nolan turned away from the body, a senior officer jumped from one of the boats. He looked to one of his soldiers down the beach who yelled back, "All clear!" The response was mimicked by one of the soldiers who went down the beach in the opposite direction.

The senior officer walked over to the three former cadets and looked at Jennee. He had seen enough death to know she had left this life. "Is anyone else hurt?" he asked.

Solemnly, Nolan responded, "No, just Jennee. The rest of us are okay."

One of the soldiers was examining the body of the assailant Nolan killed. He yelled down, "Looks like they were Toltec mercenaries!"

The senior officer shielded his eyes as he looked at his subordinate and nodded. Then he turned back to Nolan. "Any idea why these people were after you?"

"No idea," Nolan said, numbly, as the realization of Jennee's death flooded over him.

"Well, I never have been able to figure out these Toltec. We haven't had a terrorist attack on this plane in some time, and usually when it happens, the goal is a political official or a senior officer. None of you are high ranking, are you?"

Nolan's head snapped around with his eyes piercing up to the little hut where he had left her. "Deahna," he said with his legs already churning into a run toward the side of the hill.

Lukas knew where Nolan was going as soon as her name left Nolan's mouth. He moved quickly to join his friend, racing recklessly up the slope between the sharp spires of rock. Nolan, not being heedful for his own safety, rushed up the side of the steep hill with reckless abandon. As he came closer to the hut, his concern grew, as he didn't see Deahna in the window. Finally, at the hut, he rushed through the door, yelling out Deahna's name.

Lukas was only a few minutes behind his friend. He sped through the door of the hut to see Nolan on his knees. The Earthman's face was white. His eyes were wide with shock as he looked at Deahna. The blanket had been strewn to the side, and from his position, Lukas could see the lower half of her uncovered legs protruding out from behind the half-wall bisecting the small room. A pool of blood was slowly growing, the edge visible as it flowed around the stone and mortar wall.

Taking a deep breath, Lukas retrieved the blanket and covered Deahna's body. Closing her eyes with his fingers, he noticed the small puncture wound in the side of her neck. The last few drops of blood had finished trickling out the tiny hole, leaving a red line down her pale flesh. He took one last look at her before lifting the blanket to cover her face. He heard Nolan, still on his knees, mumbling, "It's my fault. It's my fault."

Lukas went over and squatted in front of his friend, grasping his shoulders. "There's nothing more you can do here. The authorities will take care of her and send her back home." Lukas was at a loss, knowing no other words or actions would change what happened.

Both men rose to their feet. Nolan was unsteady as he took one last look at Deahna, but it was as if he was in a dream. He remembered feeling Lukas guide him toward the door as a gust of wind, filled with the fresh scent of the sea, swirled through the window, circling throughout the hut. As they exited the small room into the mid-afternoon sun, Lukas scrunched his nose. He thought it odd. Mingled with the scent of death, his nose reacted instinctively to the acrid odor of burnt herbs. The thought came and went instantly. He had more urgent things to worry about as he put his arm around Nolan, helping his bond brother down the side of the hill.

Chapter 12

It was two weeks after Deahna's death, and Nolan awoke to a knock at his bedroom door. He blinked open his eyes as the lids fought the mid-afternoon sun peeking between the curtains fronting the window.

The knock came again along with Daniel's voice. "Wake up! It's late, and you are sleeping your life away!"

"Okay. I'm getting up," Nolan replied. Based on the sound of the footsteps, Nolan's words were enough for Daniel who went back to the living area of his quarters.

Nolan thought, *if only it was that easy. If only I could sleep my life away and not feel the guilt I do.* Every night since he had returned, it took hours for sleep to overcome him. The short periods of rest were the only times when his mind was at peace. When he awoke, it took only seconds for his thoughts to return to the people who had died because of him: the men back on Earth, Dragon and now Deahna. He thought, *who's next?*

It was indeed late. He lifted his head to a familiar scene. He had been out all of the previous night, wandering the streets of Bailemor while having a few more drinks than he needed, but more than anything, he looked for anyone to try and get in his way. His flippant attitude caused several arguments that luckily hadn't turned into fights. Of late, he had an *I don't care* attitude toward his life. He pulled on his robe, and walked to the kitchen area where Daniel was seated, sipping a drink similar to what Nolan knew as Earthen coffee.

Daniel raised his blue eyes over the cup's rim. "How was your night?" he asked.

"It was the same as usual. I was off learning more about the culture of Bailemor. You could call it a street-level view." Nolan poured himself a cup of the same black brew and sat at the table opposite the older man.

"What have you learned about the people of Bailemor, then?"

Nolan placed the cup on the table while his eyes flared with irritation. "I've learned Lukas is not among them. He is off in training, or perhaps he's already dead fighting this war of yours. I've also learned Deahna isn't among them. She's dead—dead because of the war, but more so, dead because of me. At least this is what I've concluded."

Daniel took another sip of his brew, his gaze deepening into the black liquid rippling within the cup. "Unfortunately, I think you are right. I had my sources check on Deahna's history. There is absolutely nothing about her that would make her a high priority target of the Toltec."

"Then tell me," Nolan said as he leaned forward. "Who did this?" His knuckles went white as his fingers held the cup tightly.

Daniel glanced down, seeing Nolan's level of tension. He had recognized the first phase of loss as sadness shadowed him for most of the last two weeks. Now, he was in the second phase, and he was angry with revenge foremost in his mind. Daniel replied carefully to his question. "There is a possibility the killing's carefully concealed motive was revenge from General Treve. Perhaps he felt taking a loved one from you would even the score, but I suspect this is not the case. First and foremost, General Treve is a warrior. If he wanted revenge, he would kill you and in all probability by his own hand. The only other logical and more probable conclusion is the Toltec from Kaezzar are still pursuing you. If you recall, their injured leader was quite incensed when we made our escape from him on Earth."

Nolan nodded. "It makes sense," he mumbled. His eyes looked up square into Daniel's. "You mentioned you have connections, and I'm sure you have many. I want you to find the name of the person responsible."

"Revenge won't bring her back. You should put it behind you and move on."

With an edge to his voice, Nolan replied crisply, "I didn't say it was open for discussion. I want a name. I have played by your rules for long enough, and I know very well you need me. You still haven't told me everything. Sure, I have strong psychic powers, but there must be much more to this story for you to take the interest you do." He leaned back in his chair. "I want the name, and if you need to justify it with negotiation, then you have that too—my continued cooperation with the Soichaint, for the name."

Daniel clenched his teeth together. He did not enjoy being put in a difficult position. After a few seconds thought, he decided he had very few options. "Very well. I will get you your name."

Nolan could see a hint of anger in Daniel's eyes, but overwhelming it was the shroud of disappointment. Nolan's shoulders sagged as he put a hand on Daniel's. "I'm sorry, my friend. I committed to you and the Soichaint some time ago, so that is a given, but please, as my friend, give me the name. I will not do anything foolish, but I do need closure on the issue."

Daniel's face twitched with a slight smile. "Then it shall be so."

The rest of the afternoon and evening were uneventful. Nolan stayed in, spending some time at Daniel's computer. He learned so much, but all the added knowledge did was give him an even greater appetite for information on the multitude of races inhabiting the endless number of worlds in the Athar. At times, he still had a difficult time with the abstract thought of the expanse. He likened the Athar to an expanded four-dimensional universe, yet he knew that all these worlds really were, were what the power of his mind, working in unison with the mind of all humans, allowed him to visualize as reality. It was confusing just to think of it, but he could not refute what he experienced since he left Earth. Therein lay indisputable evidence that, although the concept of the Athar was indeed abstract, it *was* a reality.

Nolan had another quick nap before his alarm woke him at 10:00 p.m. He washed and dressed, although he didn't select the finer clothes from his closet. On his late-night excursions, he was accustomed to wearing a weathered look. The flat-black slacks and teal-blue shirt, accompanied by the faded, gray leather jacket, suited him well.

Not long after, he was in the bullet car, scooting under the platform of the Lower City toward the main transfer station. Once there, he parked the vehicle and made his way to the larger public bullet that, in short order, had him speeding off to the entertainment district. The view out the window was familiar since he used this route several times during the last two weeks. He was under the business core of the city, where a maze of monorails was suspended in two tiers. Even at this late hour, bullets of every size and shape sped along the different tracks while the occupants were subconsciously thankful for the city's traffic computer that kept collisions to a minimum.

In less than ten minutes, the bus-like bullet docked at the Entertainment District Station. He departed the vehicle and made his way up the escalator amongst a throng of smiling Bailemorians. This is why Nolan came here. During the dark of night this area of the city stayed alive. Whether it was the restaurants, play houses, theatres or outside café's, the business of all the establishments was rooted in bringing a smile to the face of the people. Here, for a brief time, the war and death were forgotten.

Nolan skipped out onto the main thoroughfare where, immediately, the music barraged him. Just up the street, what best could be described as a funky brass band was plying their trade with fervor at an outdoor café. In the opposite direction, people were flocking out the exit from a theatre where a show had just finished. The theme music, matching the best Broadway cadence Earth could have mustered, was bellowing out speakers along the roof. It gave the audience just leaving a final, memory-provoking, subliminal stake. It also drew the eyes of other Bailemorians walking the streets, who were enticed to join the audience for the next show.

In his bland attire against the many dazzling suits and dresses rampant on the *Strip*—as this area of the entertainment district was called—no one took much notice of him. He wasn't recognized as the mysterious Earthman, now Akkadian, who won the most exciting flying event of the century. Nor did they recognize him as the man who subsequently killed the Gwyneddman who just happened to be the pilot of the competing jet. Nolan had been acquitted of any wrongdoing, but he understood the looks he received in other parts of the city when he was recognized. Everyone likes a conspiracy, and the attraction intensifies when the wholesome hero has a perceived dark streak. That's why he liked it here—where he was nobody.

Heading north, Nolan walked under the many neon signs advertising the different establishments. He inhaled deeply as he walked by different restaurants. It rekindled memories and senses, as some of the best food he ever ate was along the Strip. The combination of food, lights and music created a fair-like atmosphere, just at a more sophisticated level.

Nolan turned right into a side alley, and the sophistication level dropped immediately. The alley was dimly lit, and he moved quickly, as it reminded him of the alley where he'd killed Dragon. He looked over his shoulder several times, but didn't see anyone following. On occasion, during his past visits, he heard footsteps but never managed to sight anyone behind him. Consequently, he wasn't overly concerned. After several such incidents, he assumed it was just his mind playing tricks on him with the thought of Dragon's death still lingering. In addition, he now took a more *take it as it comes,* reckless attitude. He still carried his knife, but he hadn't carried his sword since the day it tasted Dragon's blood. *If someone wanted a piece of him, be it the Kaezzarites or General Treve, bring it on,* he thought. *Let the chips fall where they may.*

Nolan walked into a swath of light as he exited the side alley into another alley running parallel to the Strip. This alley was no more than a laneway 20 feet wide, and from there the resemblance was curtailed to a smaller, less sophisticated copy of the upper-crust entertainment area he just left. Wires crisscrossed the alley over his head, dotted with plastic lights in the shapes of various animals and birds of this world. The music here was also different, as the big band sound was left behind, replaced with the fast-paced folk music played on various stringed instruments. The more casual music brought a care free atmosphere to the *Little Strip* as this long, back laneway had come to be known.

Every few feet another merchant was cajoling Nolan in their attempts to have the Earthman come into their store to purchase cheap merchandise at inflated prices. Nolan stepped back, startled. A troubadour had just fired his batons. He threw first one, then a second, and finally a third, into the air. He juggled them higher and higher as the people of the alley made their way over, clapping in unison to spur the young man to propel the burning batons to greater heights. He was only one of the many street entertainers who made a meager but happy living plying their trade on the Little Strip.

Nolan tossed a coin into the basket beside the fire thrower before moving on down the alleyway, where he came to a small alcove cut into the side of a building. It's 30-by-30-foot area was rimmed by a line of electric lanterns. The light, playful keyboard music, playing in through the speakers situated at the corners, gave the outdoor café a comfortable atmosphere.

The alcove was filled with round tables where each was surrounded by chairs. Almost all were filled with people laughing and drinking the sweet alcoholic beverages of Bailemor. At the corner table, sitting with a group, was a barrel-chested man. He was in his late forties and had a thick build, reminding Nolan of the sturdy oak trees of Earth. His face was wrinkled beyond his years, and he carried a thick, black moustache flecked with silver. It was a contrast to his short, white hair, cut square and short at the top, reminiscent of an upturned scrub brush. The man saw Nolan and waved his hand as he yelled, "Eh Flyboy, have a drink. Come!"

Nolan smiled and made his way over. On his first visit here, the older man, surprisingly, had recognized him as the Academy contest winner. In the Little Strip, names were not important, so Nolan was nick-named *Flyboy*.

He made a path through the tables and chairs, sitting in the one pushed out by the older man's foot. "So, how is the Gypsy King tonight?" Nolan asked the man who carried his own nickname. Nolan gave it to him since the group spending their time in the café reminded him of the gypsies of Earth. They had a carefree attitude, exemplified by the smiles they always carried on their faces. Nolan also loved the accent they spoke with. Since he'd been visiting here, he discovered the people of the backstreets talked in slang.

"We es good, Flyboy. Me has en drink, and me food is done." The Gypsy King lifted his glass, filled with the sweet fermented beverage, and his other hand rubbed his belly.

"Well, I haven't eaten yet. What's good tonight?"

Duly cued, the other older men at the table all began to give advice—each with a toothy smile. The Gypsy King elbowed Nolan, then pointed to the pictures of the specials hanging above the entrance way to the inner café. "Take en number one. Never going wrong wit number one."

"Sounds good to me," Nolan replied

Before he could turn to find a waitress, the shrill voice of the Gypsy King pierced through the air. "Katrinaaaa!"

A young, dark-haired woman pushed open the door from the café, and her high-heeled walk brought her through the tables to theirs. Her hips had a practiced sway that drew the gaze of the men, and she knew it.

Once at the table, she said, "Welcome Flyboy. Katrina can git what for you?"

Nolan smiled at her. "The special. Number one and thanks."

Katrina put her hand under Nolan's chin, lifting his gaze to her brown eyes. She tilted her head side to side. "No, you still too much remember your woman. Es en shame. Now, Katrina, if you let her, could make you forget your woman es gone." She rolled her shoulder so that her breasts rubbed together, accentuating her cleavage visible over the neckline of the low-cut top.

Nolan chuckled nervously. "I think just number one."

Her hand slid down from his chin, continuing along the back of his neck and around his shoulder. Her hip rubbed against him. She laughed as she threw back her head while her hair sensuously flowed down her back. "Maybe they did en tell you. The pictures es wrong." She rubbed her hand across her lower belly. "*Number one* es right here, and it is most very special!"

The crack of flesh on flesh cut through the air as the Gypsy King's palm slapped into Katrina's behind. "Just de food, woman!" he yelled with his eyes clenched shut.

She jumped an inch into the air with the impact, causing her breasts to bounce to the enjoyment of the male clientele. She winked at Nolan and moved off to the kitchen to get his food as her hips swayed with each click of a heel on the tiled floor.

The Gypsy King clapped his hands after her. "And bring him drink already!" After a few moments, he leaned closer to Nolan. "Katrina es a good woman, but she es like to tease you. At least she show that en her face in front, but I tell you a secret. Behind that face, en her heart, she has beauty, and en that beauty, she holds en place for you."

Putting his hand on the older man's shoulder, Nolan said, "I've told you of my sadness, and it makes it easier coming here, seeing the joy you live life with. It shows me, even if I don't have everything I want in life, I can be happy—" He looked into the Gypsy King's eyes "—in time, but not yet."

The corner of the Gypsy King's lips turned down, his eyelids drooping closed in a look impressing on Nolan that the Gypsy King knew the answer before he had responded. After all, he was the Gypsy King. "So, if I cannot get en your interest en a girl, perhaps this stupid old man can convince you to gamble en lose everything you own, to me?" the Gypsy King coaxed.

Nolan raised an eyebrow. "Possibly. Let's see what the cards have to say," he said. He pulled 20 small silver coins from his pocket, placing them on the table. "But remember, if I win, then I'll be the King of the Gypsies."

The Gypsy King pulled coins from one pocket and a deck of cards from the other as he nodded his understanding. The other three men at the table, seeing the show of silver, stopped their conversation and also pulled money from their own pockets. Every night, when Nolan came here, this is how he passed his time. The ritualistic challenge with the symbolic dowries were always followed by a night of gambling. All the while, he would watch the people of Bailemor as they passed by the café—what some referred to as watching the world go by.

After several drinks and two hours of card play, Nolan felt a tickle at the back of his neck. He looked up and across the alleyway just in time to see a man quickly look down to his feet. Through the still busy alley, Nolan could see the man standing with another taller man just outside a small pub 30 yards away. Nolan wasn't sure why, but he was sure these men were here in the alley because of him. An instinct inside him compelled him to believe it was true, unquestionably.

The Gypsy King looked up from his cards. "They ev been there for 30 minutes."

"You saw them also?"

"Es sure. After all, I es the Gypsy King." He winked at Nolan. "Do you want them removed?"

"Not yet." Nolan rubbed his chin. "Let's wait and see what they do." He thought it better to be patient, as he didn't want more people killed because of him. They could be the general's men, or even worse, they could be Toltec.

They returned to their cards while only occasionally looking up to see if the men were still there across the alley. It was an hour later when Nolan noticed they were gone. He saw no more of them, so when he could see the brightness indicating the impending rise of the sun, he gave his farewells and began his trek back to Daniel's.

He was wary, looking around each corner before he moved on, and was relieved when he arrived back at the parking garage at the main transfer station. He would wish he kept his guard up a little longer. Just as the door of the bullet car opened, he felt the crack of a solid object against the back of his head. He fell forward into the vehicle, and as his face scrunched into the back cushion of the chair, he felt the sharp prick of a needle into his upper arm. Nolan didn't know if it was due to the hit on the head or the needle, but everything went black, and he lost consciousness.

Nolan awoke to the splash of cold water on his face. He pried open his eyes to find everything out of focus. He tried to bring his hands up to rub his eyes but found he couldn't, as they were bound behind his back. He gave his head several shakes to clear the fog from his mind. The room came into focus, and to Nolan's surprise, he wasn't in a room at all. The large warehouse was dark except for two small lights, one on each side of the wooden chair he was propped in.

Each light had a silver reflector pointed at Nolan, making it difficult for him to see beyond the lights. He heard movement, then a voice from the darkness. "We have some business to take care of, Nolan Harrison."

Squinting to try and see into the darkness, he replied. "I would love to participate, but I'm a little tied up right now."

Nolan heard a deep, soft chuckle from the darkness. "Through all my son's faults, he also had a good sense of humor." A shadow walked forward into the light. Nolan immediately recognized General Treve.

"I'm sorry your son is dead, but he wouldn't leave me alone. There didn't seem to be many options," Nolan said.

It was as if the general didn't hear him. "There is a consistent belief across almost every plane of existence—an eye for an eye. You have taken my son and my heir. Now you will pay the price."

Nolan's brow beaded with sweat while he unsuccessfully tried to hide the exertion evident on his face as he struggled to free his hands from their bonds.

The general paced back and forth in front of him, his fingers intertwined behind his back. "I should tell you the drug injected into your arm will temporarily make it impossible for you to focus on the Athar. Transposition will be impossible for hours, and by then, you will be dead."

"I'm not your enemy," Nolan offered.

Once again, the words passed right through the general. "But first, some introductions, then I will explain the process by which you shall meet your end." He held his hand in the air, snapping his fingers. Two men and a boy walked into the light. The general pointed to the older man. "This is Dragon's uncle." His finger slid to the second younger man. "This is Dragon's bond brother." Finally, he pointed to the boy. "This is my other son, Dragon's younger brother."

Nolan just looked at them in disbelief as the general pulled out an energy pistol and aimed it at him. He invoked his shield as the general pulled the trigger, and the burst fizzled against it.

"Yes, your shield still works," the general said. "At least for now. My brother and Dragon's brothers will fire upon you until your shield has drained. Then, as Dragon's father, I will finish you. Your debt will be paid with your blood, and hopefully, my mind will be at peace."

Nolan maintained his shield as he struggled at his bonds. He felt the tingle in his fingers—the one Daniel told him to fight. He did so now, hoping it would increase his shield's strength. All four men moved back into the darkness beyond the lights. Nolan heard the familiar sound of static as the pistols built up a charge. He saw the flash of blue, then felt himself thrown back. Knocked on his side, he and the chair were spun as the second burst slammed into him. Three more bursts came, and each one spun him and the chair. Nolan's breaths were labored. He could feel his shield weakening. His mind actually became calmer. There was a resolve in him. As much as one part of him said to give up, another deeper instinct told him he needed to fight with all his might and remain alive, as he was meant to serve a greater purpose.

Another set of bursts spun him in a circle. His head was woozy, and he felt the tingle in his fingers once again. He thought he saw a glow of light from behind him but quickly put that to his delirium. His thoughts were floating, but still he felt the strong instinct to survive as his shield sputtered out. He relaxed his thoughts. He was finished, but something inside shouted, *No!* He saw a single blue burst coming at him, and in the brief glow he saw the general's face above the pistol.

Something happened. The burst changed speed, coming at Nolan in slow motion. The view in front of him became blurred. He felt himself being pulled. He didn't try to stop it. Rather, he let his mind go.

At the back of the warehouse, a cloaked figure watched the event. His face lit up with an orange glow as he sucked on the pipe. The only indication of his shock was the slight raising of one eyebrow. The burst from General Treve's pistol smashed into Nolan or at least the chair Nolan was tied to, and it burst into two. When the smoke cleared, the bonds were still tied, but they hung slack and empty.

There was no sign of Nolan Harrison, dead or alive.

Chapter 13

General Julian Morenz stood on the large stone veranda overlooking the expansive garden ten feet below. The sculptured greenspace of 30 short, rolling hills was an eye-appealing contrast to the general flat terrain of Kaezzar. On top of each hillock of neatly trimmed grass was a small garden. Each unique garden gave life to a different theme, letting the imagination of those who gazed over it exercise the power of their mind. He looked at one dominating hillock where a tall sickle tree, brought from the forests north of Lake Fuego, grew upward with dark, twisted branches and expansive, light-green leaves. At the foot of the trunk, a ten-foot swath of velvety clover languished, content in its submission to the much-needed shade. Another hill attracted his sight with a burst of brilliant red leaves. The fire bush was not native to Kaezzar, having been brought from another plane, ten years ago. Now, it was a favorite of the elite who spent more money on their plants than most working-class people would spend on their children, but such is the case on many planes of existence. With position comes power while power draws wealth, and Julian was now beginning to reap such benefits.

Unfortunately, the breathtaking garden was not for the enjoyment of all. An eight-foot-high, stone wall kept out the prying eyes of the general public. Winding through the short hillocks, a flagstone path provided a route for the guests of the house to have a closer view of the many individual gardens.

This was the first luncheon Julian attended at the senator's home. He turned, looking upon the dwelling that was even more impressive than the garden. The hand-lain, natural, stone walls were of the same gray stone as the perimeter wall of the garden, and cutting across the walls was a row of auburn trim. There were three such rows with the upper row bordering the top of the wall, three stories up from the deck he now stood on. He panned his eyes to the left where a round tower, jutting out at the end of the fifty-foot length of wall, all but filled his gaze. There was one such tower built into each corner of the building, giving it a masculine, strong appearance. It was something he thought he fit into very well.

Hearing a slight shuffle of feet to his right, he turned his head and found the senator's wife beside him. Smiling politely, he used her formal title as he addressed her. "Madam Senator, I was admiring your wonderful home."

The madam senator pulled her lips back in a warm, velvety smile matching the tone of the day. Much younger than the senator, the glint of white teeth accented her beautiful high cheek-boned face, highlighted by unusual, green eyes, framed by blue-black hair that was straight, and shiny as silk. She tilted her head up, letting her hair sway with the sparse breeze blowing across the elevated patio. "You've been aloof today, and even now you're deep in thought. Is the mind of the youngest and most promising general troubled?" she said playfully.

Julian leaned back against the thick, wood railing supported by stone pilasters. "If there's one fault I have, it's that I do not easily leave my work behind—even when entertained by such a lovely woman."

She chuckled royally. "Well, if my presence alone cannot keep your mind from your work, perhaps you would accompany me on a walk in the garden to provide further distraction. The beauty it holds might cause your mind to stray from the serious issues of state, if but even for a few moments." The madam senator offered a slender hand covered with a white silk glove.

Julian pushed off the railing and held his elbow out on an angle. Her delicate hand slid under it, fingers curling around the thin forearm as they walked toward the stairs leading downward.

Inconspicuously, Julian nodded across the patio to Jelan Tulis who stood by the entrance to the house. The muscular man was now free of his incarceration, and Julian had employed him as his own personal bodyguard. As they walked through the hillocks admiring the wide variety of colors, the sounds of the other guests on the upper patio faded, replaced by the chirping of birds and the calming sound of a small waterfall built into the hillock they were just passing. Jelan maintained a discreet 20-pace-distance behind them.

"I see my husband has chosen well," the lady stated. "You have taken your WTF duties seriously. So, how are things coming with your efforts against the peace activists?" she asked.

"Slowly." Julian raised a hand to indicate a level of frustration. "I have many levels of clearance, but I've found things move very slowly in government circles. I finally have my staff in place, but they need to become accustomed to my pace. I have set a challenging schedule for them, so we shall see if I've chosen as wisely as your husband." He tilted his head back, letting out an artificial laugh.

They were now at the far end of the garden, following the stone path that curved back toward the house, when they both heard a vibration. The madam senator furrowed her brow. "What's that noise?"

Julian reached inside his jacket pocket, pulling out a small, portable phone as he smiled at her. "Excuse me for one moment. It seems my work is never done." Flicking the cover open stopped the vibration after which he pulled the phone to his lips. "Hello."

"Turn around."

Julian frowned. "Who is this?"

The words came slowly. "I said, *turn around.*"

Julian turned, facing the lady who had stopped in front of him. "This should only take a moment," he said to her as he covered the speaker with his hand. Over her shoulder, his eyes caught a movement in the distance. On the corner hillock, backing onto the stone wall, was a collection of high bushes. A large opening was cut into the middle of the colorful flora, and within it stood a stout, stone bench. In front of it was a pond fed by a fountain of water, curving upward from a statue. The life-size form of a clown pressed the fountain of water from its bulging cheeks and red painted lips. Through the arc of water, Julian saw a man sitting on the bench, one leg casually crossed over the other. He was wearing a black cloak—unusual for the temperate day.

The voice came through the phone once again. "Come see me. I have something for you." There was a click as the phone connection was terminated.

Julian didn't close the phone as he pulled it against his chest. Looking at the lady he said, "My apologies, but this is an important call I have to take. Its departmental business."

She smiled coyly. "Of course. I would not want to stand in the way of the war." A sweet laugh rolled off her lips.

Julian waved to Jelan Tulis who came over to them immediately. "Escort the Lady back to the house. I will be there momentarily after I take this call."

Nodding, Jelan put his hand out, palm up, indicating the Lady should go ahead of him.

Once Jelan Tulis and the madam senator were out of view, Julian snapped his phone closed and pressed it angrily into his jacket pocket. Walking briskly to the clown, he furtively looked both ways to ensure the line of sight from the house was indeed obscured. He looked through the arc of water at the man sitting on the bench. Julian's eyes were smoldering. "Peron, this couldn't wait?" he sputtered.

Peron's dark eyes casually turned up to Julian. He ignored the general's question, pointing a crooked finger to the spot beside him on the bench. "Sit."

Julian felt fear crawl up his spine as he looked into Peron's eyes. He wondered how many people saw this dark visage as their last sight before the spy smote the life from them. He decided it best to comply with the dark man's request, and he slid to the spot indicated.

Peron's scarred hand slid under his cloak and produced a small vial containing a swab stick. He held it out to Julian between his thumb and forefinger. "In here, you will find the information you are looking for."

Gingerly taking the vial while being careful not to touch Peron's fingers, Julian held it up to his eyes. "What is it?"

Peron wiped his fingers on the bench. "Within the vial you will find two DNA codes. One is female, and one is male. The male DNA belongs to your Nolan Harrison."

"That's all?"

"That is everything," Peron hissed through his clenched teeth. "Analyze it! You'll find the answers to your questions, and with that, my work for you is complete." He put his hands under him to push up from his seated position on the bench.

Julian's fingers clasped Peron's wrist. "Wait."

Peron's face snapped toward Julian's. The general saw his own death reflected in the dark pools filling the sockets on the killer's face. He knew he just made a grave mistake, yanking his hand back instantly.

Peron was tense, and his knuckles were white as they clenched the edge of the bench. His voice was barely a whisper. "My work for you is done. I've seen what the contents of the vial will tell you. This man Nolan Harrison is very powerful—much more powerful than you ever imagined. If you have any sense, when you see the analysis, you'll burn it, then put the report and any memory you have of Nolan Harrison from your mind."

"He cannot be that formidable. You obtained the DNA sample from him."

"Not from him," Peron corrected. "I took the DNA sample from his woman. He will not be pleased, and it will elevate him to become an even more formidable adversary. I sense a strength about him which tells me even what I have seen is but a small piece of what is yet to be revealed. I don't want to be there when the time does come."

"I will double your payment," Julian offered quickly.

Peron rose to his feet as he reached inside his jacket once again, pulling out a pen and paper. He scribbled some numerals onto it and thrust it toward Julian. "After you see the results of the DNA test, if you're foolish enough not to heed my advice, and you still want to pursue this man further, then you will be foolish enough to pay this ridiculous price." He didn't wait for a reply as silent steps carried him quickly around the hillock and out of view.

Julian sat for a few minutes, fingering the vial in his pocket. It troubled him that Peron appeared uncomfortable with the mission concerning Nolan Harrison. The spy was normally a cool, calculating professional, or at least that was what his contacts had told him. He shrugged it off, thinking, *I suppose everyone has a bad day.*

He rose from the bench, dusted his behind, and made his way back to the main house and the senator's luncheon. Finding the senator with his wife, he made his apologies, blaming his hasty departure on his attentiveness to his duties. The senator clapped him on the back, reassuring himself more so than Julian, that he made the right choice in having him lead the critical task force.

With the luncheon completed, Julian collected Jelan, and the two men made their way to the MagTrak station. There was very little conversation as Julian's mind was still preoccupied with the vial and its mysterious contents. For some reason, Peron was gladly rid of it as if it contained a fatal disease.

Once at the station, the pair made their way to the first-class car and sat in chairs opposite each other. Jelan looked out the window, making sure no one was following before relaxing his frame back in the soft, cushioned chair. "You seem tense," he said to Julian.

"No more than usual," the general snapped back. "It's nothing you need to worry about right now."

Jelan put an arm up on the back of the chair. "Where are we going?"

"Back to Central High Command. I have some urgent business there."

Jelan nodded but didn't respond. He had been with Julian long enough to know the man. He was usually talkative to the point of being obnoxious, but when he spoke in the curt sentences he was using now, Jelan knew Julian's mind was elsewhere.

Julian's body swayed to the right as the MagTrak began its deceleration under the Eye of the city. It took the two men only a few minutes to move to ground level and arrive at their destination. Two soldiers in black uniforms, laser rifles slung over their shoulders, stood at attention on either side of the opening in the eight-foot-high, iron-railed fence.

Julian turned to Jelan. "I will not need you for the time being, but keep your phone on." He pulled out his photo identification, showing it to one of the guards who let him pass through into the inner courtyard. Passing several other officers of the mainstream military in their solid black uniforms, he felt the power of his position, enjoying the way they looked twice at the yellow trim on the collar of his maroon jacket. In his mind, it was a distinction putting him above them all.

There were four large, plate-glass doors fronting the four-story structure. Julian moved through the doors on the right and into the security checkpoint where another soldier watched as Julian swiped his identity card. The green light indicated the mainframe computer's acceptance of the card, and the soldier waved him through. Normally, Julian would go up to his office on the third floor, but today, when he entered the open doors of the elevator, he pressed the button taking him to the basement and the laboratories located there.

With a pneumatic *whoosh*, the doors slid open, and Julian walked out into the brightly lit hallway. A sign on the wall opposite the elevator doors caught his attention, whereby he brought his nose almost in contact with the sign as his fingers traced down the index of rooms. "Where is it? Where is it?" he mumbled the repetition.

Two military nurses walked by him with bemused looks on their faces as Julian blurted, "There it is!" while rapping his finger on the sign - *Genetics Suite B31*.

A small arrow beside the listing indicated the destination room was to his left. Julian turned in that direction, checking the suite number of each doorway, counting them down—29B—30B—and, finally, 31B. Walking in through the entranceway, Julian found himself in front of a waist-high counter. On the other side was a man facing away from him, diligently at work, keying data into a computer. Julian waited a few moments before clearing his throat to catch the man's attention.

The man didn't turn around. He just pointed behind him and to the right, barely missing a stroke on the keyboard. "If you have a request, put it in the bin on the counter."

Julian's face creased into a frown. "I do have a request for a DNA test—"

The man shot his arm out again, pointing to the in-box.

"—with a level six security priority," Julian added.

The tapping on the keyboard stopped. The man spun around in his chair and pulled the bifocals down his nose, peering at Julian. His other hand moved to his mouth, his finger and thumb stroking down from the corners where a curly moustache joined into a thick, light-brown beard. The lab technician considered Julian, catching sight of the yellow collar. He rose to his feet on the other side of the counter. "WTF business, eh. Who might you be?"

Julian was impressed the man recognized the new War Task Force uniform. Placing his identification card casually on the counter, Julian slid it within the lab technician's view. "General Julian Morenz," he quietly replied.

As the man peered down, Julian squinted because the glare from the lights reflected off the bald man's head. The lab technician, well into his fifties, looked up at Julian and then down at the picture on the card. He repeated the process several times. Finally, the man looked up and said, "People here call me Doc. What can I do for you?"

"Well, Doc," Julian eyed the man up and down as well, "I need this sample tested right away." He reached into his pocket and handed the vial to the older man.

"What is it?" Doc asked as he held the vial up in front of his face. He gave his head a quick shake, coaxing the glasses to slide down, back onto the bridge of his nose.

"I said this was a priority six request. As such, the results will be confidential."

Doc's face momentarily contorted with irritation. "Well, come on then. Priority six states you need to watch everything I do." He walked around the corner of the wall into the main laboratory area.

Julian followed Doc, lifting himself up onto a stool. With his feet dangling, he had the appearance of a student waiting for class to begin. He watched Doc prepare the sample and place it in the test chamber before he slid into a seat in front of another computer. It took some time for the sample to be processed. Julian waited impatiently while Doc attended to other work with his fingers methodically tapping the keyboard.

Doc swiveled the chair around as he addressed Julian. "You'll need to put in your access code."

Julian slid off the stool and leaned over the desk, looking at the video screen. Beside the words - *Level Six Security Access Code,* he typed in his password. As his fingers finished typing on the keyboard, in large green letters, the words - *Clearance Approved,* flashed on the screen.

Doc pointed to a printer behind Julian that had just whined into commission. "Your report is coming off now."

"All other records are being erased?" Julian asked.

Turning the video screen so Julian could see more clearly, Doc pointed to the lines of text scrolling down the screen. The last line came up with the message - *All Files Erased.*

Julian moved to the printer and pulled the single piece of paper from the tray. The paper was almost at eye level when he hesitated, pulling the sheet against his chest. He looked at Doc who had an inquisitive look on his face. "If you don't mind, wait for me in the other room."

The look on Doc's face changed to one of disappointment, but he arose from the chair and disappeared around the corner of the wall without saying a word. Julian walked over to the stool. He put one foot on the lower bar to raise himself high enough to slide onto the seat, and at the same time, he pulled the paper in front of his eyes. At that moment, his mouth fell open and his foot slid off the bar. He toppled to the side, catching himself with his hand on the countertop beside the stool.

He snapped the paper back in front of his eyes. He read the results again, then a third time. Each time the inspection was more detailed until the final viewing consisted of Julian moving the paper mechanically across his field of view, line by line. There was one result for female DNA, just as Peron had foretold, but there were seven lines containing the results of the test on Nolan Harrison's DNA—seven lines where there should have only been one!

Impulsively, he crumpled the paper up in a ball. No wonder Peron was so visibly shaken! What he saw on the paper was just folklore—an old tale told to children before they went to sleep. It couldn't be true, yet he couldn't refute the results of the test. *This is a much bigger issue than I ever imagined.* He was correct in doing the test within the highest security clearance. If this information became public, who knows what the extent of the consequences would be.

With his fingers shaking, he unraveled the report and ripped it into tiny pieces. He pulled one of them up, realizing he could still read partial words. Turning his head from side to side, he sighted the burner on the far countertop. He put the paper shards in a metal bowl he found beside the burner and fiddled with the air flow and a cinder flash until the burner was emitting a thin, blue flame. He tipped the bowl until one piece of the report caught fire, quickly spreading to the other shards.

The small flames reflected in Julian's eyes. His mind was spinning as he pulled the piece of paper, he received from Peron earlier in the day, from his pocket. Peron had a choppy, crude stroke befitting his trade. Julian considered the number for a moment and agreed with the spy. The monetary figure was ridiculous, but Julian knew he would pay it. He would pay even more if Peron asked it. What he saw on the DNA report needed to be eradicated—completely. He looked again at the now expired contents of the bowl, pushing the ashes from side to side, ensuring nothing legible was left. Just as the report was no more, Julian knew Nolan Harrison must also be terminated. He and all who knew the true nature of his power must be carved from the Athar. Nolan Harrison was once again at the top of his list.

Chapter 14

Darkness. That was all Nolan saw from his curled position on the ground. He was completely disoriented, his chest heaving with deep breaths as his mind recounted the last few moments. His shield had dissipated. Then, the blue burst of energy from General Treve's rifle shot toward him, and finally, shear panic had set in. Oddly, for a split second, his mind rewound to the last time he felt the panic of having his life in danger. Thoughts of the flying competition, and his near deadly flight through the haze-coated, dead city flashed into his mind.

It was at this point when he felt himself drawn by the Athar. It was as if a doorway opened in front of him. By now he'd hopped to different planes numerous times, but this one was different. He put it down to the drugs injected into his blood. In the panic, it was inconsequential. All that mattered was that he had avoided certain death at the hands of General Treve. If he would have stayed, he knew he would be a dead man, so he let himself go. Anyplace would be better than letting the general have another shot at him.

He propped himself up on his hand. It took several minutes to recount the events from the time at the warehouse to his present unknown location, knowing in reality the time for the events to unfold could not have been more than a few seconds. That is all the time it would have taken for the energy burst to reach him. Seeing the burst come toward him, he thought *surely his end was here,* but the severe ache in his chest told him he was still alive. Although his shield protected him from a lethal blow, it didn't stop the bruising effects of the impact. As his senses cleared, he turned his head from side to side, realizing he could not see more than a few feet in any direction. It was not a pure pitch-black darkness, but a dark-gray similar to a fog-filled night. He took a deep breath, choking on the air he tried to pull into his lungs. Bringing his hand up to cover his nose and mouth, he took another breath—this time with more care. The air was thick and filled with suspended particles. Pulling off his jacket, then his shirt, he ripped a strip off the bottom. He tied the long, eight-inch-wide swath of cloth around his face just below his eyes before securing it with a sturdy knot behind his head. He took another deep breath, satisfied and relieved the cloth served effectively as a filter.

Nolan rose to his feet, hoping that a higher vantage point would give him better insight regarding his location, but he was disappointed to find this was not the case. He pulled his jacket back on and almost lost his balance with the effort. The lack of directional orientation played tricks on his mind, confusing up from down. *Why did I hop to this plane?* he thought. It didn't have to be a plane with a beach and a warm climate, but at least sunshine would've been a convenient consideration.

His mock self-pity was interrupted by a glow in the distance to his right. As he watched the brightness, he realized it was moving toward him and quickly. The brightness covered a wide front. Even if he wanted to run, the effort would be in vain, as he couldn't see to his left or right. With very few options, he pulled himself down prone on his stomach, waiting for the brightness to come to him. He thought of Daniel. His friend had always been there in the past when his situation appeared desperate. He wished he was here now along with his knowledge and wisdom. He would know what to do.

Just before the brightness hit him, he instinctively closed his eyes, expecting the worse, but the worse didn't come. All he felt was warmth on his back. He pried open his eyes and rose to his knees. Looking up, he searched for the source of the illumination and found it far above him. He saw the round outline of a sun surrounded by dark shapes.

"Freaking hell," he whispered. "It's just the sun coming out from behind a cloud."

At least now he could see 30 yards in every direction, although he might not have wanted to as there was nothing of consequence to see. The ground was a combination of small pebbles and rocks on a flat terrain visible as far as he could see before the more distant perspective was swallowed by the mist. He focused on the fog surrounding him. It was thick and almost stuck to him as he moved. He waved his hand downward, watching it cut through the vapor sludge, leaving a turbulent swirl. *Nasty stuff,* he thought as he once again considered his next course of action. He tried to pull the Athar into his mind, but he couldn't. He thought it odd since he had hopped here, but he put it down to the unstable nature of the drugs that had been forced into his system.

Suddenly, it was obvious. The sunlight refracting down through the thick mist revealed its true color—red. He snapped his watch in front of his eyes. Built into it was a compass, and the needle was pointing to his left. As he pressed the small button on the side of the dial, the compass point swung around as it was neutralized. When Nolan let the small button go, once again the needle spun and pointed to his left. He repeated the exercise two more times with the same result. He was shocked. There was no magnetic pole on Crann Bith, but many years ago the scientists placed a strong electromagnetic device in the heart of Bailemor. In the event someone was lost on the planet, the compass would always point to the city, giving them a directional reference. He realized this mist was not a mist at all. The red haze indicated he was still somewhere on the surface of Crann Bith!

Still somewhere between confusion and shock, following the direction of the compass, he turned his steps toward Bailemor. He actually made good progress. Even though he could only see a short distance in front of him, the terrain continued to be flat and without obstruction. However, his mind kept coming back to his transposition, although he was beginning to doubt it was a transposition at all. Hopping, by definition, was from one plane to another and purebloods couldn't hop from one place to another on the same plane. That was called *teleportation* and everyone knew only the Anasazi owned that skill. It was their gifted power. Also, in the back of his mind, he remembered the words of General Treve. He had been given a drug so he wouldn't be able to hop from the confinement of the warehouse, but somehow, he had. He scratched his head. Even now, he couldn't yet invoke the Athar in his mind, so how did he hop? The only conclusion was he did not.

Nolan walked for hours along the bleak terrain, and it gave him too much time to think. He mulled the facts over and over in his mind. By the time he saw the large shadows in the distance, he knew the truth. He had teleported to this location. Now concluded, it was something he decided to put from his mind until he saw Daniel, at which time, he would have some pointed questions to ask his friend and mentor.

He concentrated on the shadows in the distance that grew larger and larger as he moved closer. They provided a foreboding scene in the eerie quiet of the red haze. His steps became even more wary as he saw their massive size towering hundreds of feet into the air. What at first appeared to be some type of rock formations, were in fact old, crumbling buildings. As he walked carefully among them, the terrain also changed, where piles of rubble had turned into smooth hills over time. With all his senses piqued, he continued onward through the buildings toward a droning pulse he could now hear in the distance. He walked toward it, being careful not to veer too close to the buildings where there were signs indicating loose pieces of rubble still fell from the heights.

Turning a corner of what was once a street, he heard the pulsing drone become much louder. He walked carefully since he didn't understand why an electrical device would be out here in this barren, long-dead city. Nolan skirted from one rubble pile to the other until he felt as if he was right on top of the droning sound. He flashed his face from side to side, trying to pin-point the location of the noise. Finally, he slowly lifted his face, peering directly above him. A hundred feet in the air was the marker used for the flying competition. It was still here since it's automatic stabilizing motors received just enough power from the solar cells powered by the partially obscured sun.

Nolan fell back, laughing. He knew exactly where he was. He was in the Dead City! What a relief. With luck, a day's walk to the west would have him at Bailemor. He was hungry and thirsty, but even if he could find these items out here, he dared not eat or drink, not knowing the poisonous affects they might have. Sitting upon the hill of rubble, he rubbed his eyes. They were beginning to sting, both from the red haze and the tiredness he suddenly felt. He also recognized the sun was going down, and in the darkness, travel would be impossible. He needed to find some cover and a place to sleep for the night. With his strength rejuvenated, and with some luck, by tomorrow evening, he would be at the foot of the city he now called home.

He looked from building to building. Any of them would do, but the doorway to his left led into a smaller and undoubtedly safer structure. It didn't seem so imposing an image, having resisted the elements and time better than most of the other buildings surrounding it. On his way to the doorway, he picked up two sharp-edged stones. They would do nicely in providing a spark, and if he could find some dry tinder and wood, he could easily make a fire to keep the chill from his bones.

Peeking into the doorway, he inspected the interior as best he could in the reducing light. There was another doorway across the room, and a soft glow radiated from it. Gingerly, he stepped toward it, bracing himself with his hands against old tables and chairs dotting the room. Holding the door jamb with both hands, he slid his face into the far room and found it was not a room, per say. It was a large atrium, three floors high and capped with a large glass dome. Several panes of the dome were broken, but it didn't affect the diffused light filtering down into the wide area.

The contents of the atrium had withstood the test of time. There were bookcases dotting the floor, and books covered the walls from the floor to the three-story-high ceiling. He realized now that the atrium was actually an old library. This would do nicely. He had at least some light and lots of material to burn in a fire. He almost jumped for joy when he saw the large brick fireplace on the far side of the room. The sun was going down quickly, so he would have to hurry before he was caught in the darkness of night. He made his way over to the fireplace, picking up pieces of wood which had once been parts of chairs and tables. The iron-meshed doors fronting the fireplace grated open, and he placed the wood into the deep opening. On the mantle, he found some tinder in a sealed box which had miraculously survived both time and the elements. He pulled it down in front of him, and with the two stones sparking together, he quickly had a fire roaring in the fireplace.

Nolan's run of good fortune continued. He searched through a cupboard along the wall and whooped with joy as he found several old cushions and blankets. Although they were old, they were better than the hard floor for his night of sleep. The last thing he did before lying down was pull at least forty thick books from the shelves and place them beside the cushions. Lowering himself under the blanket, he practiced with a sacrificial book which must have been a text book, considering its weight. With an easy toss, it hit into the fire, throwing a large flame up into the air while casting giant shadows against the far wall. *Excellent,* he thought. He had but to toss a book or two in the fire every hour or so. It should allow him to get the sleep he needed for the long walk ahead of him tomorrow.

He threw two more books into the flames, then almost a third. However, the gold-raised lettering on the book caught his eye, and he blew the dust off the leather-bound cover. He handled it carefully, appreciating the detail. It was from a time before cassettes and discs, when the experience of life and knowledge was expressed in an artistically written form.

However, it was the name emblazoned in gold letters on the front that piqued his interest. It read - *The Tale of The Three Keys.* The words unlocked recesses within Nolan's mind, relieving the frustration there that had been in the background for some time. It came to him that Daniel, and even Germaine, referred to him several times as the *First Key* and a key to the Soichaint movement. His curiosity got the better of him, so he didn't throw the book on the fire. Rather, with great care, he opened the cover and began reading.

The kyng sat on the meager wooden bench in the castle tower with his eyes looking up at the nyght sky, pondering the past. As it was on most nyghts, his thoughts wandered to events long unfulfilled. Inevitably, his mind backtracked to the source of his discontent, rooted in the creation of humankynd. The war and death having crisscrossed the layers of humanity, from tyme on end, was a heavy burden on his heart, and even now distracted him from the brilliant yellow and red colors lyghting up the nyght sky.

The kyng of kyngs remembered those days long past as if it was yesterday, recalling his own feeling of being incomplete. The canvas of creation needed more than color, sound and smell. It needed lyfe. So, on that fateful nyght, he wandered from the castle, and there, from the seven points of his crown, he created the seven races of man, giving each a unique power. Each power was formidable in its own ryght, but the true strength of man would come when the powers worked in harmony, sacrificing individual goals for the better good of a cohesive mankynd.

But alas, it had not been so. Greed, vanity, dishonor and untruth drove the seven races of man apart, and war was forever on their lips. It often irritated the great kyng. He even considered wiping the creation from the volume of the Athar, but he reminded himself he was not left here by the old ones to be rash or act in haste. He considered it patience more so than stubbornness that held his hand in check. The burden to oversee the Athar was one he bore with pryde and determination. It did not allow him to give up easily.

That brought him to this nyght and the realization his devised plan would be played out. He had decided humankynd would be given one last chance to decide their destiny. Man would need to trigger the process which would bring them from the darkness and back into the harmony of peace he hoped for them.

The kyng's determination moved his feet, carrying him down the long wynding staircase. His bones creaked, not having moved him from his lofty bench for centuries, but it was time to act. His resolve motivated his steps, bringing him to the emptyness in front of the castle. With a magical movement, sparkling dust sprinkled from his fingers. The energy touched by the dust followed the old kyng's silent command, turning naught to matter. As a result, he felt the comfort of soil and grass materialize under his sandaled feet.

His eyes looked from left to right as rays of pearl-white lyght emitted from the empty sockets. Raising his arms, the robe fell back to his elbows. He moved his lips, chanting words of old. The expanse of energy hovering over him began to churn in a wide circle. On each cycle less lyght was seen, and a billowy, black cloud filled the void vacated by the lyght.

The kyng opened his eyelids, smiling as he felt the wynd blow through *his whyte beard, knowing the spirits of the old ones fueled the wyld motions of the air. His own movements were fluid, and the façade of the old kyng was revealed as he moved in unison with the wynd. His lips mumbled a chant from a time before life as his hand, palm down, passed before him. Appearing in the wake of his movement was a human infant, eyes closed in its unborn, virginal state.*

The kyng whispered, "Man itself is the First Key, but not just any man. Instead, one who will show all the races can live together in harmony, even if their blood be different." With that, the kyng raised his fist to the wynd and yelled, "The elements of all lyfe will course through this child—behold!"

A bolt of blue lyghtning struck into the ground beside the great kyng, showering particles of light and matter high into the air. The kyng's hand moved again in a backward motion across the front of his body. The wyld wynd obeyed, sweeping down from left to right, blowing the storm of elements over the infant. As his hand came to a stop, his other hand raised a fist to the sky. Once again, his voice bellowed over the wynd. "Ancient ones, bring me fyre!"

A great fyreball appeared above the old kyng, plummeting toward him. Raising both arms straight in the air, he yelled an ancient incantation. The wyld wynd instantaneously reacted, swooping down, blowing the kyng's robes hard against his body before turning up to split the fyreball in two. One section of flame consumed the infant, annealing the elements of man to his body and then tumbled off into the depths of the infinite Athar. The second fyreball slammed into the ground beside the kyng where the elements of life were still suspended in space. There was a resulting great explosion of lyght when the fyreball hit, absorbing what was left of the elements. The sound of steam assaulted the old kyng's ears, but it did not deter him. Through the seething, hot myst, he reached down and picked up the two-headed hammer that had been forged by this fyre of life. He noted the seven lines circumscribing the head before placing it, handle down, into his belt.

His fist shot into the air for a third time before the steam could dissipate. His eyes of lyght looked upward, beseeching, "Lords of Old, bring me rain!"

With that, the black, billowy clouds let loose their torrential load. What was left of the steam sizzled as the droplets passed through it before pelting into the ground. Looking down, the kyng saw the rain pooling blood-red between his legs. Pulling a vial from his robe, he reached down and scooped up the red fluid of life, holding it up to the wyld wynd as it swirled over him.

The kyng, now sodden from rain, walked over to the infant and took up a position straddling over it. "Proof all the races can coexist in the same body—that is the First Key!" He then scooped up the infant, and the wynd swirled around him before the kyng's hands pulled back. The wynd took over, drawing the child away and propelled him into the depths of the Athar.

The kyng's hand pulled out the hammer of life, hefting it twice before again looking up to the sky. "The chemical formula that resides in the lines will let humankynd reproduce coexistence. Here is the Second Key!" His arm pulled back, then sprung skywards, sending the hammer tumbling end over end until it was lost from syght, deep in the Athar.

The vial being the last object he held, was now pressed upward in his crooked fingers. The kyng looked at the blood-red fluid. "The blood of the races lies in this vial and shall never be lost, hence, the Third Key!" It was sent following the hammer, whistling as it sliced through the Athar.

Sighing with his work complete, the kyng felt the currents of air caress him. He was now alone with his thoughts. "It is now out of my hands," he muttered. The destiny of humankynd lies with the humans. He felt his beard flutter against his chin as the wyld wynd still circled around him. The feeling soothed the old kyng, but he knew what he had to do. "Caretakers of time, givers of lyfe, follow the Keys and protect them." He raised a hand to the Athar, and the wyld wynd caressed him one last time before sliding up his arm and off his fingers. The kyng watched for some time until the swaying motion of the wyld wynd was lost from syght.

"Farewell, my friends," he whispered. Then he turned, walking somberly back into the confines of his castle, weary from his unsettled peace.

Nolan closed the book and placed it on his chest. Intertwining his fingers behind his head, he looked up at the glass dome. "It couldn't be," he mumbled. Daniel and Germaine referred to him as the First Key, but this was only a fairytale—nothing more than a children's book. Surely Daniel couldn't think he was this being of superhuman power that carried the blood of all the pureblood races in his veins. He chuckled as he thought, *my mind must be playing tricks on me. The drugs and the ache in my chest must be having some serious side-effects.* His mind went back and forth, mulling over the facts. He knew his powers were very strong, and he couldn't explain the teleportation just the day before. His eyes went back to the book, and he laughed once again. "This is freaking crazy," he muttered through the laugh as he rubbed his eyes. Truly, his weariness was driving his mind to exercise the full extent of his foolish imagination.

The laugh turned into a yawn. It had been a long day, and he was still feeling the effects of the blasts from General Treve's laser rifle. If he was, in fact, this savior of the people, it could wait until tomorrow. Daniel will know what to do. With that thought, his eyes closed, and he fell immediately into a deep sleep.

From the dead calm of the night, a breeze blew down through the broken glass dome. It curved over the fire, raising the embers back into flame, then shifted over the book still on Nolan's chest, rustling the pages. Nolan did not wake, so he didn't hear the whispering voices as the wind circled over him before trailing off into the distance.

Chapter 15

A low rumble awoke Nolan from his slumber. Unable to pry open his eyes, he bolted upright in a panic. The panic was quickly replaced by relief as he wiped the caked layer of red sediment from his eyelids. Even though the rumble seemed to come from all around him, a quick circumspection told him the source of the noise was from above. Rain was pelting off the glass dome, and the excellent acoustics of the book-lined room echoed the prattle into the multi-directional rumble he heard at floor level.

He pulled the remnants of his shirt from his face and took a deep breath. Cleaning the rag as best he could in the red haze filling the room, he then tied it back securely around his head. Some of the rain made its way down through the broken glass panes of the dome, giving the atrium a dampness that didn't help the aches he already felt from a restless night of sleep.

Picking up the last four books from the pile he made the previous night, he tossed them on the red embers within the fireplace. The dry, aged material caught almost instantly, and the warmth brought some relief to the dampness having worked its way into his clothes. He picked up the book that had fallen off his chest and for a moment considered throwing *The Tale of The Three Keys* on the fire, but he had second thoughts. Although he didn't like what the words might imply, the fault was not with the book. The reading, after all, allowed him to fall asleep, albeit a restless one, so he carefully placed the book back amongst the many others on the dusty shelf. He chuckled, thinking, *perhaps in another century another man will find the book on the shelf and compare his life to that of the infant and foolishly be left wondering.* This morning, his senses were alert and stable, and he looked at the other books on the shelf, rubbing the dirt from the label stuck to the shelf under them. Wiping the grime off the tag, he read the words - *Children's Favorites.* "That's all it is," he mumbled, "a children's fairytale."

The surprising sound of yelling coming from the distance shocked Nolan. He quickly doused the fire and made his way through the two doorways leading him toward the street. Carefully, he poked his head out, looking in both directions. The yelling did not repeat, but what he did see still amazed him. The rain was falling in a heavy downpour, beating down most of the red haze. A thin layer still filled the air, but he could easily see a hundred yards in any direction. However, at ground level there was a thick, soup-like, three-foot layer of compressed haze. It kept trying to rise, but the rain pelted it over and over, giving it the appearance of a boiling broth as the surface of the thick layer billowed and popped.

He heard it again, drawing his eyes up the street to his right. Men were yelling in the distance, but this time, it was closer. Out of the haze, he saw three people appear, running toward his position. There were two men, and well in front of them, a young woman. As they came closer, he could see the fear on their faces, especially the girl who was much closer. She was quick as the wind, and although her legs were shorter, her lithe form bit through the air with amazing speed.

Looking further up the street, he saw what they were running from. Two heavily-armed men were riding them down on trosks. There was both a spear and sword strapped to their saddles, and he could see a laser rifle slung tightly over each of their shoulders. One of the men carried a bow with the arrow cocked and the twine pulled taught, ready to let loose. The rider's fingers curled out, and the arrow whistled through the air. There was a sickening thump as one of the men fell forward, lost to sight in the red soup.

The remaining man and the woman turned their heads for a moment, but only a moment because the fear for their own lives outweighed the concern for their fellow runner. The man turned sharply and raced up a side street, followed by one of the riders. The other rider continued after the girl as her wet, red-tinged hair blew behind her in the mist.

Running and not being able to see the ground was difficult and proved to be the woman's undoing, as she finally stumbled and fell into the red soup, directly in front of the doorway Nolan was peeking out of. She rose and tried to run, but fell to one knee. She was injured and Nolan saw the look on her face from his hidden position. Her fear had turned to defeat. The rider continued forward, having cocked another arrow. It let loose and accelerated toward the woman.

Nolan reacted instinctively. His conscious mind watched as his shield flared into life. Extending his hands toward the girl, the shield leapt out in a flare of energy, and the arrow ricocheted off his shield, disappearing into the thick layer of red haze.

The rider, his face filled with surprise, looked toward Nolan who had come out from his concealment to face the oncoming trosk. The girl didn't move. The appearance of another man surprised her, but she recognized the stranger had just saved her life, so she remained frozen, unsure what to do next. The rider's look of surprise turned to one of fury as he put his heels into his beast. Simultaneously, his hands fumbled with the rifle as he attempted to sling it from his shoulder.

Once again, Nolan's instincts took over. He felt the tingling on his fingers, the tingling Daniel told him to always suppress, but this time he did not do so. He let the feeling build, and he looked down at his hand, seeing a pulsing globe of orange energy form on his fingertips. His shield was still glowing around his body, and the two energies merged, causing the energy sphere on his fingers to turn a bright purple.

He knew what to do, and his hand let loose the purple burst. It flew toward the rider even as he ducked to try and dodge it, but his focus on the rifle slowed his reaction time. The rider's shield flared into life at the last second, saving his life, but it didn't prevent him from being thrown off the trosk and flung against the wall of the building, ten feet behind him. The trosk was also wounded, running off into the distance, wailing pathetically.

Nolan held his hand out to the girl and said, "You have two choices. Take my hand and come with me. If you do, you will live, or stay here and die." Nolan laughed at himself. He realized those were the same words Daniel had told him when they had first met on Earth.

The girl, seeing this was not the time for a debate, took his hand, and they both turned back to the doorway Nolan had previously come through. She flinched, but Nolan pressed on her hand as she tried to dart away. Another man stood in the doorway ahead of them, and he had a thick, blonde moustache under a familiar wide-brimmed, leather hat.

"Daniel, what on Earth are you doing here?" Nolan blurted.

"Crann Bith, not Earth," Daniel replied coolly.

"You know what I mean!" Nolan cried.

Misinterpreting Nolan's raised voice, the girl moved closer against him, sliding her hand up his arm until it locked on his elbow like a vice.

"Come this way. We need to move from this location since there are more riders." Daniel waved his hand, urging Nolan further into the building.

Nolan followed Daniel for the time being, putting his curiosity at Daniel's appearance aside. The woman tagged along, more by her grasp on his arm than any intention he had of bringing her. With Daniel in the lead, they walked through the building they were in, crossed another narrow street, and then continued through the length of another long, narrow structure. At the end of it, they were at another doorway Daniel warily poked his head through. As he peered up and down the street, they heard the sound of several horns in the distance. After several minutes, he pulled himself back in the doorway, facing Nolan and the young woman.

"It appears there are at least 20 trosks with riders and another ten or so men on foot. They are moving by our present position, back toward the area of the attack." Daniel did not wait for a response. He poked his head back out the door with his hand held out behind him. He suddenly waved it forward as he whispered, "Now." With that, he was in a run across the next street through the rain that was still pelting into the red haze.

Nolan followed quickly, feeling the tug on his arm as the girl hung on frantically, legs spinning under her. They sped through a doorway into the next building, continuing after Daniel who they saw running up a staircase—two steps at a time. After several more flights, they found themselves on the roof of what now revealed itself as a narrow but tall structure. From this higher vantage point, Nolan could see numerous trosk riders milling up and down the streets in the area they just left. As he looked over the other three sides, he saw one or two riders in each location. They were surrounded!

There was a small structure on top of the building. It was two-sided with a corrugated roof that had withstood the test of time. They took cover under the lean-to where Nolan turned to Daniel, finally asking, "How did you find me?"

Daniel pulled off his hat, shaking the water from it. "You called me."

"What do you mean?" Nolan responded, a confused look on his face.

"I am not sure I understand it myself," Daniel replied. "Yesterday morning, when you did not come home, I had some concern for your welfare. However, in the later morning I had a strong sense of you in my mind. I knew you were in trouble, but for the moment safe. I also knew you were still on Crann Bith, and I knew your exact location."

"That's crazy. We aren't telepathic."

"Correct. *We* are not, but it would appear *you* are. I cannot explain the mechanism of how it happens. I just know I had an overwhelming feeling that your mind reached out to me. You know those feelings you get where you sense, with an absolute certainty, that something is so. With the first connection, Germaine and I hopped to another plane. Last night, I felt the second connection and hopped here."

Nolan shook his head, not wanting to accept the truth.

Daniel put his hand on the younger man's shoulder. "There is something I have not told you—something I now need to reveal."

Nolan sarcastically chuckled. "Is this where you tell me I'm the First Key, and I have the power of all the races given to me by some almighty king-creator, so I may save humankind from itself?" He rolled his eyes as the words slid off his lips.

Daniel was left open-mouthed with his eyebrow raised as he gained a new admiration for his young disciple. "Yes, something like that, but it would seem I have little to add."

Nolan maintained the sarcastic expression on his face.

Daniel squeezed his fingers on Nolan's shoulder. "I believe, although the tale is just a tale, it is rooted in truth. You have powers far above any other pureblood. Your shield is strong, and I saw how you threw it from your body to save the girl—a feat impossible for any other Celtae. The fireball you threw proves you also have Toltec blood flowing in your veins. Your teleportation mimics the Anasazi and your telepathic powers, although crude, show you have the blood of the Shang mixed in your veins."

"You always make it sound so simple," Nolan said as his shoulders slumped. "I don't think I'm ready for this. All I want right now is to go back to Bailemor and put on some dry clothes."

Daniel's hand slid off Nolan's shoulder. "We can't return there, at least not for some time. Although General Treve cannot make public his attempted murder, he can twist the tale to meet his own needs. He has done so, and now all of Bailemor suspects you are an Anasazi spy. They also think Germaine and I are your accomplices. At this time, it would not be wise for us to return there."

Trumpets blared. The riders in the streets below were coming closer in their search. Daniel moved out into the rain, peeking over each side of the roof, then he scurried back into the lean-to. "We don't have long before they search this building."

Lowering an eyebrow, Nolan asked, "Exactly who are 'they?'"

Daniel shrugged, and his face showed signs of embarrassment. "I know they are Akkadians since they wear the blue earrings. There have always been rumors of the *Hunt*. It was a sport many centuries ago when purebloods hunted scull prey. Outlawed many years ago, we have seen first-hand evidence it still exists in secret." It was then that his eyes turned to the young woman.

Nolan also turned to her. In all the commotion this was the first time he had a second to really consider her. He held her by her shoulders and asked, "You're injured. Can you continue to travel?"

Wide-eyed, the girl nodded up and down.

"What's your name?" Nolan asked.

The woman looked from one man to the other, but her gaze finally rested on Nolan. "Ranaa. My name is Ranaa."

Her voice was soft. Even though her hair was drenched in a red layer of wet paste, he could tell the locks underneath were blonde. They hung just past her shoulders in the back and were roughly cut shorter at the sides and front. Nolan had difficulty taking his eyes from hers. They were unusually beautiful, owning a color he had never seen before. They were olive colored but spotted with bright-yellow, giving the appearance her eyes were golden. They sparkled even in the dim light on this rooftop.

Finally breaking the gaze, Nolan looked her up and down, seeing the long scrape running from her knee up her thigh. In the light-red mist of the rooftop, neither the girl nor Daniel could see his blush that came since this was the first time he noticed she was near naked. Ranaa had a rag around her waist which passed for a very short skirt, and her breasts were barely covered by a tattered shirt open at the midriff. The only other thing she wore was sturdy leather sandals. *At least they gave her that,* he thought. The riders wanted the chase to be competitive.

The trumpets blared again, and now they heard voices from the street directly below. "We are out of time and need to hop from this place now," Daniel urged.

"What of the girl?" Nolan asked.

"All three of us together will surely get caught. She will have to fend for herself. She is quick. If we go now, she has a chance to sneak between the riders."

"To where?" Nolan blurted.

Daniel's brow furrowed. "We don't have time for this debate."

"I won't leave another woman behind to die." Nolan's thoughts flashed back to Deahna.

Daniel thrust his hat on his head, bending a knee in a stance showing his frustration. He thrust a finger in Nolan's face, and his words were rushed. "Alright, there is another option. You were able to throw your shield around

Ranaa once before. Do so again, and as long as you keep your shield between you and her, you will be able to hop and carry her safely in your wake."

Nolan's face twisted into a foolish, confused state. "You always told me we couldn't carry other energies with us, and that includes sculls. We will both die!"

Daniel roughly grasped Nolan's arm. "You are different! Long ago, our ancestors could do this. At least that is what our history books tell us. Our powers faded with some interbreeding, so now we can only shield ourselves, but it is quite obvious you have the ancient powers."

"Where are we going?" Nolan snapped.

"Iswan. That is where this journey ends, and a new journey begins with you as the First Key. You go first, and once you have successfully hopped, I will follow." Daniel moved his hand to place it on Nolan's shoulder so he would know Iswan's location in the Athar.

"No need," Nolan said, having peeked into Daniel's mind. "I have it." He pushed Ranaa a few feet from him as his shield came to life. He said, "Don't be afraid. I won't let anything happen to you. Just close your eyes."

With his words, the fear dispelled from her eyes and she closed them, placing her hands calmly by her side. Nolan moved the shield around the woman, ensuring the void between the two of them was completely filled with the green energy. Then his mind looked into the Athar, and the beacon Daniel called Iswan lit in his mind. He focused on it. Daniel watched as a wide oval began to ripple, first around Nolan, then it spread around Ranaa. Daniel was impressed. The oval was huge—proof again that Nolan did indeed have the power. Their figures first obscured and were subsequently lost in the ripples. Finally, there was nothing left but swirls of red haze.

Daniel waited a few moments until he was hit with a sense of Nolan in his mind. *Yes, he was safe.* He knew the younger man would send him a message indicating he arrived safely. Footfalls on the stairs interrupted his thoughts. The riders would be here in a few moments, so he invoked his own shield. As he did so, he thought of Nolan Harrison—the First Key. Humanity had a chance. The man who he met almost a year ago, in the forests of Earth, was in many ways the same. His deep-rooted morals and knowledge of right and wrong, were really what gave him potential to wield the powers for the side of good, for he knew if Nolan's powers were misplaced or misled, he could wreak havoc on all the pureblood races. Daniel's ever-growing confidence in the young Earthman gave him hope for his people and all the pureblood races.

Several men burst up onto the rooftop. They saw Daniel's rippling oval begin to fade. Pulling their rifles, they fired a flurry of blue energy at the man, but by the time it reached his location, he was gone. They thought it ironic the man in the oval, so near to coming to his end, had such a satisfied smile on his face.

The story continues in Wyld Wynd Unleashed, book three of the Wyld Wynd Series.

Dear Reader:

Reviews are important to every author. We are thankful that many readers take a few moments to return to the purchasing website, in this case, Amazon, and leave a rating and a review.

If you could do so for this story, it would be much appreciated. Keep in mind, a Hollywood style review is not needed. Even a few simple words would be great.

Thanks again, and I hope you enjoyed the story.

Peter Sandor.